Excerpt from Love Those Hula Hips

The music slowed and the emcee crooned, "And now, ladies and gentlemen, a tribute to all those in love, performed by our very own Ho-ku-lani."

At first, James thought he was seeing things. The woman from the lobby moved across the stage in such a fluid motion, he thought she might be an apparition. She positioned herself not more than six feet from him. He leaned back in his chair and stared at this dark-haired beauty. She seemed to acknowledge his gaze with a slight nod and a sly smile, and then began her dance. "Ho-ku-lani," he repeated to himself.

Mesmerized by Hokulani's onyx hair and matching dark eyes, he tracked her flowing mane to her undulating hips and gaped when she stood in front of him. Her smile was magnetic and her hands delicate, but the way she moved her hips captivated him the most. He needed to know more about her.

Love Those Hula Hips
Jackie Marilla

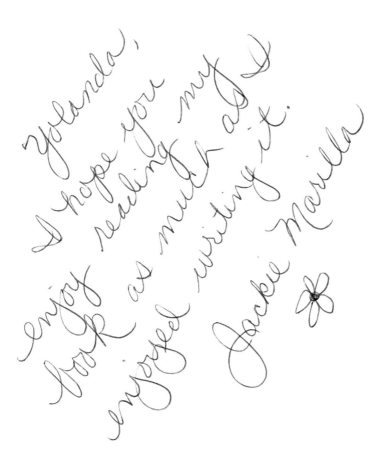

Yolanda,
I hope you enjoy reading my book as much as I enjoyed writing it.
Jackie Marilla

Copyright © 2014 Love Those Hula Hips

Books to Go Now Publication

All rights reserved

ISBN-13:978-1499615272

ISBN-10:1499615272

DEDICATION

Mahalo nui loa to the Sundae Writers' Group (Darlene, Kris, and Lora). Without the support of these women, this book would still be a collection of disjointed scenes. They encouraged, critiqued, edited, listened, and talked some sense into me when I needed it. I love you all.

Chapter One

I don't want much, James Westerman thought as he stared out the window of the 737. *A business to run and the chance to win Father's competition. This investment could be my ticket to both.*

The parched air slapped James's face as he exited the plane and walked down the metal stairs to the sweltering tarmac at the Kona International Airport. He shaded his eyes with the Wall Street Journal and followed his lawyer, Sam Sagal, and the other first class passengers to the luggage carousel.

"Fifty-six degrees warmer than Boston," Sam commented.

"And five thousand magnificent miles away," James said.

They gathered their bags and hailed a cab. On the fifteen-minute ride to the property, James mentally recorded his first impressions. To his right, the onyx-colored landscape, interrupted by buildings and flowering bushes, gave way to the sapphire and sea green of the Pacific Ocean. Upland, clouds gathered over the hillside and houses dotted the landscape. When they turned onto Ali'i Drive, James rolled down the window to inhale the brine of the ocean and feel the breeze on his face.

As the cab pulled into a ground level parking area, James assured himself the Kona Breezeway Inn was the property he needed to prove to his father he was as good a businessman as his older brother.

James and Sam entered the drab, chestnut-colored lobby decorated with hieroglyphics of some sort. The brown-toned couches, with their frayed cushions and arms of broken down wicker, looked like tired old bag ladies. The men got in a long line of people waiting to check in. Only one woman stood behind the counter, and it appeared she wrote every registration in longhand.

James craned his neck to see beyond the other guests. Not a computer in sight. *So much for efficiency*, he thought. *No wonder this place isn't making it.*

Just then, a dark-haired woman with flowers in her hair waltzed across the lobby and greeted the guests. "Aloha. *Mahalo* for waiting."

When she passed by James, a floral fragrance perfumed the air. He gazed at her as she walked behind the counter and began to assist the desk clerk. He noticed the smile that never left her mouth and the voice that soothed his taut nerves, but he especially noticed the way her floral print dress hugged her hips and breasts as she walked out from behind the counter to place a flower lei on each guest and give them a brief kiss on the cheek.

"This is taking forever," Sam mumbled.

"What?" James asked without taking his eyes off the woman.

"I said this is taking forever."

"Enjoy the view." James nodded toward the counter. "Remember, we agreed to enjoy the property as guests today."

James waved a family of four ahead of them in line.

"What are you doing?" Sam asked through clenched teeth.

"Manipulating the line so we get checked in by the woman with flowers in her hair."

"Here's a little free advice, James. Don't start with a woman already. You know how it distracts you."

James ignored Sam and continued to monitor every move of the alluring woman. When it was his turn, he approached her with the confidence of someone sinking a putt two inches from the hole. "James Westerman," he crooned.

She smiled and sashayed around the counter. While the provocative scent of flowers coaxed his head forward, her delicate hands reached to place the plumeria flower lei. When her fingers grazed his earlobes, he fought the urge to wrap his arms around her and draw her irresistible body to his.

"Aloha. Welcome to the Kona Breezeway Inn, Mr. Westerman. Enjoy your stay."

"I'm sure I will."

****

Hokulani Kawelu performed the duties at the registration desk like a robot. Greet. Smile. Welcome. Memorize the name and face. She forced herself to maintain that demeanor until all of the guests registered. When she left the lobby and walked down to the haven of the cultural center, she finally allowed her smile to evaporate as she dropped her face into her hands.

A month ago, her family received a foreclosure notice for the Breezeway. If they didn't find an investor soon, they would lose the inn and the sacred Hawaiian land it sat on.

Hoku shook herself. She needed to believe a positive outcome would present itself.

She glanced at her watch and decided a swim in the ocean would help to relax her. She changed into her suit, wrapped a sarong around her hips, and hurried down the walkway to the beach that fronted the property.

Hoku entered the Pacific with an audible sigh. She swam just beyond the wave break and turned to lie on her back. The familiar up and down cradling motion of salt water eased the tension at the base of her neck. She closed her eyes. As the waves rocked her back and forth, her arms and legs relaxed and her spine melded with the ocean. Her lips formed a crescent of contentment as images of growing up at the Breezeway emerged like a slide show—her grandmother stringing plumeria leis for the guests, catching *'a'ama* crab on the beach with her brother, and her mom weaving *lauhala* leaves into baskets. Hoku's throat caught as she imagined her beloved dad playing "'*Opihi* Man" on the ukulele while she danced a lively hula.

A sharp but familiar whistle from the shore broke her reverie. She opened her eyes, rolled over to her stomach, and swam toward Kawika. With each stroke, she prayed her brother found an investor so they would not face foreclosure. They needed to hold on to the Breezeway. Dad would have wanted it that way.

"Aloha." Hoku wrapped her sarong around her waist and planted a kiss on her brother's cheek.

"Aloha, Hoku. Good news. I just got a call from a possible investor. He wants to meet with us tomorrow morning."

Hoku threw her arms around him.

"Whoa! Don't get me wet." He held her at arm's length.

"I knew you'd figure out a way to keep the Breezeway in the family."

"Let's just take one step at a time." He dropped his arms to his sides.

"What can we expect at this meeting?" Hoku asked.

"I faxed the financial statements last week, so the investor knows we can't meet our obligations. He drafted a proposal, so he's done his homework and is still interested. But it's not a done deal, Hoku."

"What can I do to help?"

"There isn't much we can do until we hear what he offers. We should all review the financials before the meeting. Mom will meet with us at nine and the investor at ten."

Hoku nodded. "This means a lot to me, Kawika."

"I know. Just let me do the talking tomorrow, okay?"

****

James took a walk around the seven-acre oceanfront property after he scheduled a meeting with the owners. He followed a walkway that led to a small, white, sandy beach tucked between rocky beaches. James looked up and down the coastline. This looked like the only place along the shore with easy access to the ocean. His head bobbed up and down and his mind whirled when he recognized the potential of this real estate.

"Going in?"

James turned to see a bare-chested Sam behind him with a towel slung over his shoulders and swimming trunks that hung to his knees.

"I'm a pool kind of guy," James said.

"There's a luau here tonight," Sam said. "I reserved two VIP seats for us."

"Sure. Might as well see how this place runs an event. Could be telling."

"Meet me at five at the luau grounds," Sam said before he plunged into the water.

James turned back toward the inn and thought about the woman from the lobby. A few nights with those hips would go a long ways. He continued his walk around the property with the hope he would bump into her. By four-thirty, James gave up his search and went to his suite.

He dressed for the luau in slacks and a blue rayon camp shirt. He felt pleased when he approached the luau grounds and saw at least fifty people in line. Sam waved to him and they fell in line with the others. Two women, dressed in aloha wear, collected tickets and presented woven ti leaf leis. They escorted VIP guests to the photo booth where James and Sam stood on either side of a hula girl who wore only a coconut shell bra and grass skirt.

After the photo, James and Sam chose seats at the table closest to center stage. A waiter brought a tray of mai tais served in carved out pineapples brimming with skewered cherries and pineapple chunks. Paper umbrellas bobbed next to the garnish.

"Very Polynesian," Sam announced.

"Very…" James paused. "Something. More like hokey."

Sam took a long pull through the straw. "Mmm," he said, "hokey never tasted so good."

James tasted the drink. "You're right. It is good." He chuckled when he reached into his pocket to silence his cell phone and felt his metal room key.

"What now?" Sam asked.

James examined the key. "It's like we took a trip backward in time. We'll definitely need to replace these metal keys with computerized room cards when we modernize."

Sam scowled. "Don't get too cocky. You haven't acquired this place yet."

"Ah, but I will."

"Yeah, I suppose. But will this property be the one to beat David?"

"Oceanfront property in Hawai'i will win over a weather-worn lodge in Colorado, don't you think?"

"You know what I really think?" Sam asked. "I think this property just might be the one you've been looking for. I think if you keep your head in the game this time, you actually will earn more profit than David. I think you just need to focus on business and avoid distractions."

James concurred. He wondered, once again, why his father wouldn't just divide up his fortune between his sons like most other wealthy parents? But no, Arnold Westerman couldn't just hand over his fortune to his heirs.

Right after James graduated from college, Arnold devised this idiotic competition to pit his sons against one another. Every three years, Arnold selected a new property for each son to manage. The son who showed the most profit at the end of the cycle received two hundred and fifty thousand dollars.

David won the first two rounds. And yes, for the most part, the properties were equivalent, except James got stuck with the one nearest Boston both rounds so his father's constant cross-examinations overshadowed his efforts. At least James and David didn't let the competition cloud their relationship.

This round, David convinced their father to let them choose their own investments. James knew he could prove himself and win if he only had some autonomy from his father. The investment in Kona was as far from Boston as he could get and still be in the U.S. He simply *must* make this work.

At the invitation of the emcee, James and Sam joined the other participants as they gathered near an underground oven, called an imu. They watched as two young guys, dressed in loincloths and rubber flip-flops, shoveled away a mound of dirt and lifted up a massive chicken wire basket covered in several layers of banana leaves.

As if to assure the guests that their main entree was actually under the banana leaves, the young men removed the steaming leaves to expose a whole pig. One of the men reached into the cavity with long silver tongs and methodically removed four steaming round rocks. They transferred the whole pig onto a four-foot long wooden tray with handles extending on either end. As the men hoisted the tray onto their shoulders, the emcee announced that the *kālua* pork would go to the kitchen to be shredded and salted before they all enjoyed it for dinner.

James admitted the pork smelled delicious, but he felt more than a little leery of eating meat cooked with leaves and dirt on top, and rocks inside.

At serving time, James scoffed at the buffet line. "You'd think the VIP guests would get their food plated and served."

"Because we're so darned special?" Sam asked.

"You know what I mean. At least we get to go through the line before too many people cough on the food."

Sam shook his head and handed James a plate.

James read the labels next to each dish and selected only dishes he recognized: a little chicken, some coleslaw, sweet potatoes, a dinner roll, and a slice of pineapple upside-down cake.

Sam mocked him when they sat back down. "Way to embrace the experience."

"I'm here, aren't I?"

By the time the hula show began, James felt relaxed from a generous amount of food and just a little too much alcohol. He hadn't felt this carefree since his college days.

The first dancers moved onto the stage and performed a rousing dance from New Zealand. Next, a sort of fashion show took place with a young lady who demonstrated at least a dozen different ways to wear a pareo.

"Who knew a girl could make a big square of fabric look so good?" James mused.

The music slowed and the emcee crooned, "And now, ladies and gentlemen, a tribute to all those in love, performed by our very own Ho-ku-lani."

At first, James thought he was seeing things. The woman from the lobby moved across the stage in such a fluid motion, he thought she might be an apparition. She positioned herself not more than six feet from him. He leaned back in his chair and stared at this dark-haired beauty. She seemed to acknowledge his gaze with a slight nod and a sly smile, and then began her dance. "Ho-ku-lani," he repeated to himself.

Mesmerized by Hokulani's onyx hair and matching dark eyes, he tracked her flowing mane to her undulating hips and gaped when she stood in front of him. Her smile was magnetic and her hands delicate, but the way she moved her hips captivated him the most. He needed to know more about her.

Just as he reached for a gulp of his mai tai, the dance ended, and four more women appeared on stage. The announcer introduced the performers and said they would each choose a partner to help them with the next dance. The women fanned out into the crowd and started to select their partners. James felt Sam nudge his arm and realized that the dancer called Hokulani walked toward them.

She leaned in close to James. "Mr. Westerman, will you be my partner?" She extended her hand.

"Only if you call me James." He leapt to his feet and took her hand as she led him up to the stage.

The dancers quickly tied grass skirts around the men's waists. Hokulani reached around James to secure the skirt and whispered, "Just follow my lead. It's all in fun."

The announcer told the men to face their partners and mimic the movements of hands, feet, and hips. James stared at Hokulani's face when she began to move her feet from side to side.

Little shrieks of laughter escaped from her charming mouth as she reminded him to try the moves. "Don't be shy."

I won't be, James thought. *Don't you worry.* He shifted his stubborn feet back and forth, back and forth, until Hokulani nodded her approval.

Next, she added a simple arm motion, and James mirrored the move. Just as he congratulated himself for his expertise, the tempo increased and her pendulous hips shimmied faster and faster until James's gaze stayed below her waist and his arms and legs froze.

Hokulani lifted his chin and looked into his eyes. She took his hands and placed them on her hips. When she gripped the crest of his hips, he smacked his lips and raised his eyebrows.

"Ready?" she teased.

More than ready. His hands smoldered and his groin ached. *Way past ready.*

The drummer slowed the pace.

Boom! Hokulani simultaneously thrust her hips and used her hands to propel James's hips sideways.

Boom! Her hands urged his hips in the opposite direction, but her eyes stayed fixed on his face.

Boom! James tightened his grip. Her hands grasp more firmly.

Boom! Boom! Boom! Hokulani's hands flew up over her head. He could not keep up with the rapid surging of her pelvis.

The music ended to the roar of the audience's good-natured laughter and applause. Reluctantly, James removed his hands from her hips. As Hokulani reached around him to untie the hula skirt, he murmured, "Are you available?"

"Yes."

Just then, the other dancers whisked Hokulani off stage. The emcee thanked the men and sent them back to their seats.

"She isn't married," James announced as he sat down and wiped his forehead on his handkerchief.

"How do you know that?"

"I didn't see a ring, so I asked her."

Sam glared at him. "What are you doing?"

"I'm enjoying the moment and thinking about how nice it would be to get to know that hula dancer better."

"She's gorgeous all right, but she's exactly the kind of distraction that will cost you your prize money. Remember, you are here to conduct business."

"But tonight is not about business, is it?"

When the show ended, James noticed the hula dancers on the sidelines posing for pictures with the guests. He stood in the line nearest to Hokulani.

Sam shook his head. "I'm going to bed."

James stepped up to the dark beauty and took her hands in his. "Thanks for choosing me as your partner, Hula Hips. I had a great time."

She brought his hands to her hips once more. "It's all a matter of timing." She swayed one way and then the other.

He shifted forward until his mouth was at her ear. "Could we meet somewhere?"

Chapter Two

Hoku laid her pointer finger on the irresistible dimple below James's lips and whispered, "Meet me in the bar in fifteen minutes."

She left the photo line and went back to the dressing area to change out of her ti leaf skirt and coconut shell bra. Hoku brushed her hair and sighed when she remembered the way James looked at her when she stepped onto the stage. He awakened a dormant fervor she hadn't felt since Martin.

She felt ready to be with a man again—especially this man. She couldn't believe she hadn't noticed his sexy dimple when she registered him. She was lucky she remembered his name, given her degree of stress earlier in the day.

Now, she thought, *I can stop worrying about the threat of foreclosure and have a little fun.*

Hoku spritzed herself with jasmine cologne and slipped into her dress. She stood in front of the full-length mirror and examined her image. The scoop neckline accentuated her full bust and the straight skirt highlighted her waistline. She smiled. No one had ever called her Hula Hips. For the first time, her ample hips made her feel sexy.

Hoku walked across the *lū'au* grounds through the service door of the Breezeway kitchen. She felt anxious to share her good news with her best friend.

"What's up?" Tatiana asked as she took off her apron and gave Hoku a hug. "That glow in your cheeks isn't from dancing. You look happier than I've seen you in a while."

"Kawika found an interested investor. We're meeting with him tomorrow."

"That's great. I can't imagine the Breezeway going out of business."

"I know. I'm so relieved. I don't know what I'd do without this place. It's all I've ever known— that and hula."

"And I can't fathom working in any other kitchen, so let's hope this guy invests."

Hoku glanced at her watch. "Listen, I have to go. I'm meeting someone in the bar."

"You're going on a date? Anybody I know?"

"His name is James Westerman. He's a guest."

"Wow. You haven't even looked at another guy since Martin. Are you sure you want to start with a guest? He probably won't be here for more than a day or two."

"I know, but wait till you see him. His eyes are the richest green I've ever seen and he has the most adorable dimple on his chin." Hoku applied fresh lipstick and gave Tatiana a hug. "I'd better go. Wish me luck."

"You don't need luck. Just be your wonderful self."

Hoku went through the swinging door to the combination bar and restaurant. She saw James seated in a booth, head turned toward the main entry. The sight of him made her as impulsive as a gambler. She strutted over to him and slipped into the brown vinyl booth until their bodies touched.

Marianna, the waitress, greeted them with eyebrows raised and chin tucked. "Aloha, Hoku. And who is this?"

Hoku introduced her to James before they ordered drinks.

When Marianna left the table, James turned his full attention to her. "Do you go by Hoku or Hokulani? I've heard you called both."

"You're very observant. My mom calls me Hokulani and I use that name for performances and business. My friends call me Hoku."

"And what shall I call you, then?" James laid his hand over hers.

"How about Hula Hips? I like the way that sounds." She turned her hand to entwine her fingers in his. The feel of his skin against hers made her anxious for more.

"How many nights a week do you perform?" he asked.

"Oh." Suddenly she felt tongue-tied. "We, uh, our *hālau* performs five nights a week."

"*Hālau?*"

"Oh, sorry. *Hālau* is technically a long house where we teach hula." She laughed. "Or store canoes."

"I think you said our *hālau*. So do you own the hālau?"

She looked at James and appreciated the way he listened to her. Without question, he came on to her, but he still listened. She tried not to babble, but seemed unable to stop. "When we say *hālau*, we usually mean the people who perform hula together. I teach hula and other cultural classes here at the Breezeway."

"Ah. A woman of many talents."

Hoku took a sip of her drink. "How long will you stay?" she blurted.

"At least a week."

"Any plans?"

"A little business and I hope more fun. A quick couple of meetings and the rest of the week I'm free. What about you? Do you ever give private tours of the island?"

Hoku considered his request. James wanted to see the island. Not once had Martin shown interest in seeing the island sights. "I might be able to show you around on Tuesday."

"And tonight, Hula Hips?" he pulled her hand to his mouth and lightly kissed her knuckles.

Hoku slid two fingers over his lips and rested them on his dimple. The invitation tempted her, but if she followed this guy to his suite, she knew she'd regret it. She owed it to her family to be prepared for the meeting tomorrow and she hadn't reviewed the financial documents Kawika left for her. She closed her eyes and sucked in her breath. "I can't tonight. Will you call me tomorrow to make plans?"

****

Sunlight crept through the space between the draperies. James opened his eyes, rolled to his side and patted the empty space on the other side of the queen-sized bed. With an audible groan, he tossed the floral print blanket to the side. *Tonight,* he thought. *I'll get her here tonight.*

For now, he needed to get ready for the meeting with the owners and woo them with his investment savvy. He gathered there were no other interested parties, but he didn't know that for sure.

James pushed the drapes aside and stepped onto his second story balcony. At eight in the morning, several small boats already bobbed in Kailua Bay. Sunlight glinted off the Pacific and turned the water into an endless jewel box. James wanted to wake up to this every day for the next three years. He vowed to acquire this property. The only other options were properties out east, and he felt positive he wouldn't last another year under the critical eye of his father.

James joined Sam for breakfast in the Breezeway restaurant.

"Morning, Lover Boy," Sam said.

"I wish."

"Just as well, James. Let's at least get through the negotiations before you start with a woman."

"You sound just like my father."

"Yeah, well maybe your father's right."

"About what exactly? You said yourself that I can beat David this time."

"I said you can if you don't get distracted."

"I deserve some fun," James snapped.

"Give it a rest. First get this deal closed and then see if you have time for a woman."

James shook his head and removed some documents from his briefcase. "All right. We'll offer to front cash to cover the fourth quarter expenses. And we need to factor in repairs. How soon can we get an inspection?"

"One, two days. We know the roof needs replaced."

"Let's take the standard twenty percent equity. We'll add a couple percent to cover the cost of the computer system and the roof. Did you check how long it takes to get a title report?"

Sam answered, "Two days for an expedited report."

James nodded his head. "Good. We might have this sewn up by the end of the week." He looked at his Rolex. "We'd better order if we want to finish before ten."

****

Hoku paused at the door to her mom's office. She resisted the need to silence her cell phone. As anxious as she felt to receive a call from James, she intended to concentrate on this meeting with her mom and brother. She ran her fingers over the wooden nameplate which still bore her dad's name.

"We should've changed that months ago," Kawika said from behind her.

"Mom wasn't ready," Hoku replied.

"Yeah, I know. Shall we do this?" He opened the door to the office and followed Hoku inside.

"Aloha," she called to their mom.

"Aloha." Roselani looked up from behind her late husband's massive teak desk. Invoices, file folders, and the checkbook covered the surface.

"What are you doing, Mom?" Kawika asked as he closed the door behind him.

"I thought if I looked over these invoices and made a new budget that we may not have to take on an investor. I don't understand how I let this happen."

"We've been over this already," Kawika said. "We'll lose the Breezeway if we don't come up with some money quickly. Let's just go over the financials and hear what the investor has to offer."

Hoku added, "As far as I'm concerned, taking on a silent partner is the perfect way to keep the Breezeway and avoid foreclosure."

The family pored over the documents until they heard three solid raps on the door.

"Here we go." Kawika stood to open the door. "Gentlemen," Kawika said, "please come in. I'm Kawika Kawelu, the family lawyer and Roselani's son."

"Nice to meet you, Kawika. I'm James Westerman and this is our family lawyer, Sam Sagal."

Hoku's spine stiffened.

Kawika continued, "Hokulani Kawelu, the Assistant Manager."

She forced herself to stand and greet James. He stepped forward and extended his hand.

"Hula Hips? You didn't tell me you were part of the Kona Breezeway Inn family." He winked and squeezed her hand.

Sam cleared his throat.

Hoku shifted her weight from one foot to the other. "You didn't ask."

"Am I missing something?" Kawika asked.

Hoku muttered, "Mr. Westerman and I met last night. He attended the luau."

"Hoku tried to teach me how to hula." He gave his hips a little shake and Sam rolled his eyes.

"How wonderful that you got to experience first-hand how we entertain our guests here at the Breezeway," Roselani said.

"And this is our mom, Roselani Kawelu, General Manager," Kawika continued.

"It's a pleasure to meet you, Mrs. Kawelu." James reached across the desk to shake her hand.

James smiled and Hoku fixated on kissing that adorable dimple. She blinked a few times then reached to straighten the cluster of orchids in her hair.

Kawika invited the men to sit down. James chose the chair right next to her. Hoku folded her hands and stared at the blue bowl with floating gardenias on the corner of the desk. She could not look at James and think about business at the same time.

"Shall we hear your proposal, Mr. Westerman?" Kawika asked.

"Certainly." James opened his briefcase and handed a bound proposal to each family member. The sheer weight of the documents intimidated Hoku. She tried to scan the Table of Contents to familiarize herself, but her finger stopped on the section titled Management Agreement.

James directed the group to the summary. "In brief, provided the final inspection of the property is consistent with the initial report, we are prepared to invest enough money over the next thirty-six months to get the Kona Breezeway Inn financially stable and do some renovations. In exchange, you sign over at least twenty percent of the assets. It's our policy to appoint a designee from our corporation as the General Manager—"

"B-But, Mom is the General Manager," Hoku stammered.

James turned his head and looked directly into Hoku's eyes. "With all due respect, Ms. Kawelu, in order for our family to invest in the Kona Breezeway Inn, we must insist on making the management decisions. We don't function as silent partners."

She sucked in her lips and dropped her gaze.

He turned away from her and continued, "Our corporation focuses on boutique hotels. Typically, our investments operate in the black within three years. If you decide to sell anytime within the next ten years, we maintain first right of refusal to purchase based on market value."

Roselani stood. "Your offer is very generous, Mr. Westerman. We will consider your proposal and call you later today if we agree to continue the negotiations."

"That's a good idea, Mom," Hoku said. This meeting couldn't end soon enough for her. She needed time to think without James in such close proximity.

James snapped his briefcase shut and stood. "Shall we say ten tomorrow morning if your family is still interested in negotiations? And let's start with the walk-through."

Hoku and Roselani nodded. "Ten is fine," Kawika said.

James followed Sam to the door, paused, and turned to address the Kawelu family. "While you're reviewing the proposal, keep in mind that it looks as though you'll have difficulty making payroll this month without financial support. I'm able to transfer funds within twenty-four hours of signing an agreement."

As soon as James closed the door, Kawika chastised his sister. "What were you doing with Westerman last night?"

She kept her voice as even as possible. "I'm not sure what you think happened, Kawika. He's the guest I chose for the audience participation set."

"And in the bar afterwards?"

"Hmm. The coconut wireless is certainly active around here." *She should have known*. "We chatted for a while after the luau. Nothing more."

"Can you negotiate with a clear head? I saw how he squeezed your hand and the way you looked at him. I thought you wanted to make this work, Hoku. I'm busting my butt trying to help save the Breezeway and now you might screw this up for all of us."

"Kawika. *'Ihi.* Respect your sister. She explained what happened." Roselani scolded.

"*Mihi.*" Kawika apologized, but his eyes betrayed him.

Roselani laid her hands flat on the desk and announced that the family would meet again tomorrow morning at nine.

Hoku looked down to place the proposal documents in her bag. She could feel the intensity of her brother's gaze.

"Please just keep away from him," Kawika said.

"I will respect your wishes, Kawika, for the sake of the family."

****

James arranged his towel on a chaise lounge that faced the calm Pacific. The pool area needed some tile work, he noted, but the pool looked adequate. There were lap lanes for those who wanted to exercise and a connected shallow pool for those with small children. James considered the addition of a hot tub and scrutinized the area to see where it would best fit.

For the third time since the morning meeting, he dialed the number Hoku wrote on a napkin the night before. When he reached her voicemail again, he simply said, "James here. Call me."

James decided to check in with his brother, David, and see what the competition looked like for this round.

James listened as David gave him the laundry list of needed renovations to make the Colorado lodge profitable. "We can get this lodge for a song, dump about a hundred thousand into wiring and paint, and make a million. My initial work here is finished. Do you think I should come to Hawai'i to help seal the deal? I can be pretty charming, you know."

"Come if you want, but I think once I get the attorney son to agree, the women will go along."

"Women?"

"A mother and a gorgeous, hula-dancing, daughter."

"Think with your brain, little brother, not with your southern body parts."

"You know I will."

As James laid down his phone, he caught movement out of the corner of his eye. He saw Hoku rush down the walkway to the beach, her green and yellow sarong exposing one luscious thigh. James called to her, "Hey, Hula Hips. Good afternoon."

She paused and turned to look in his direction.

James headed toward her.

"I hope you're enjoying your stay, Mr. Westerman."

"Please drop the formality, Hula Hips. Call me James."

"I'm more comfortable calling you Mr. Westerman under the circumstances. And please don't call me Hula Hips."

"Hmm. You thought it was pretty clever last night. And it is so apropos." He put his hands on her hips. She brushed them away.

"You should've told me you were in town to invest in the Breezeway," Hoku muttered.

"Like you said at the meeting—it didn't come up."

"I need to go."

"Have you checked your phone messages? You agreed to show me some of the sights."

"That was before I knew who you were."

"I don't see how showing me some of the island violates the negotiations." He touched her hands and shrugged his shoulders.

"This has nothing to do with you personally. It's what you represent. Please understand why I can't." Hoku turned and walked away.

James watched her until both glistening hips disappeared into the ocean.

Chapter Three

The next morning, Hoku arrived at her mom's office right at nine. She knew Kawika probably reviewed every detail of the proposal after he got home from work last night. The family needed James. He was the only investor who'd shown any interest in the Breezeway, and they had less than a month before the bank foreclosed. She smoothed down the skirt of her dress and took a deep breath. She hoped her brother could offer a solution that would appeal to James and still allow the family to maintain management decisions for the Breezeway.

Roselani and Kawika were already talking when Hoku entered.

Kawika cleared his throat. "It comes down to this—if we insist on maintaining management decisions, we need to offer something substantial in return."

"What do you think, Mom?" Hoku asked.

"I know your dad would vote to hold on to the Breezeway at any cost. We have a legacy to protect and a promise to Hanalei's ancestors." She wiped away tears with the back of her hands. "We vowed to use the *'aina* as a place of cultural awareness and that is a solemn promise for generations to come—for your daughter, Kawika, and your future children, Hokulani."

Hoku turned to Kawika. "Do you have any idea how to accomplish this?"

"We don't have a lot of choices, and I don't think Westerman will give up management easily, but I do have a proposal that might convince him to share management with Mom. Westerman likes his money, so I propose we increase his holdings from twenty to twenty-five percent. We'd maintain some of the management of the Breezeway, but we'd also be forever in his debt."

"We are already forever indebted to the legacy of this land, Kawika. So be it." Roselani folded her hands on her lap.

Hoku closed her eyes and took a cleansing breath. "And what do you see as my position, Kawika?"

"I see you continuing with the entertainment contract and the cultural classes. You'd have more time to develop the *hālau* if you weren't involved in the business decisions. Maybe even have time to enter the Merrie Monarch Hula Competition like you always dreamed of doing."

"So now you are defining my dreams?"

"I'm just saying, Hoku. We're compelled to come up with a reasonable proposal. Do you have a better idea?"

"No. I trusted you to come up with a proposal and you have. It didn't occur to me that you see me only as a performer for the Breezeway."

"I didn't mean it that way. Maybe I should've just let you try to save this place."

"*Mai hana kuli,*" Roselani scolded. "Quiet yourselves. We must find a solution together, not tear one another down."

"I meant no disrespect, Mom." Hoku hung her head.

Kawika continued. "The Westerman Corporation has an excellent track record for turning around boutique hotels within a three-year window. To do that, they expect to control the day-to-day operations to cut corners where possible so the business grows. We just need to convince Westerman that the Breezeway is so unique that any mainlander would require assistance with the management."

"I know," Roselani piped in. "We should take him on a tour of the island. Help him understand our position by sharing our cultural roots."

Hoku jumped in. "I offered to show him some of the sights. We should introduce him to Madam Pele. I could take him to the volcano today."

Kawika looked like he'd explode. "I thought you agreed to stay away from him."

"I have stayed away, but I thought we wanted to introduce him to our culture to help him understand the Breezeway's appeal."

"Hokulani and I will take him," Roselani said. "You cannot object to that, Kawika."

He threw his hands into the air. "I'm just trying to get a deal made, Mom. That's what we all want, right?"

Hoku and Roselani yielded to Kawika.

"Then let me run the negotiations."

"What do you want me to do then?" Hoku asked. "Just listen and sit like a spectator who doesn't understand what's going on?"

She wondered why Kawika resisted her help in the negotiations and why he so adamantly wanted to keep her away from James. And then it occurred to her.

"That's it," she mumbled.

"What's it?" Kawika asked.

"Are you trying to protect me from a mainlander?"

"I thought we were talking about the negotiations, Hoku."

"I'm asking, Kawika. Is this about me getting involved with someone from the mainland?"

"Look. You were so unhappy for so long after Martin. And I can see that Westerman is interested in you and you in him. His life is on the mainland, Hoku."

"And my life is here. I know. I appreciate your concern, it's just that—"

"It's just what?"

"Never mind. I don't want to compromise the negotiations in any way. The most important thing is to keep the Breezeway in the family."

"Okay, then." Kawika resumed his instructions. "Mom, you take charge of the walk-through and share the history of the Breezeway. And Hoku, if you think you can persuade Westerman that understanding our culture is integral to the success of the Breezeway, offer to take him and his lawyer to the volcano."

Hoku knew she won a round with her brother, but in her heart, she also knew she betrayed him. While she believed that exposure to their Hawaiian culture might change James's mind about shared management, if she was honest with herself, she craved his attention and time with him away from her brother.

****

James and Sam arrived at the office at ten, and in a matter of seconds, Roselani looped her arm through James's and led the entourage through the lobby and down the walkway to the beach. She stopped about halfway between the walkway and the shoreline before she spoke.

"My Hanalei saved his money when he served in the military. This land, our 'aina, belonged to his great-grandmother who received it from a member of the

Hawaiian royalty as a gift for saving the life of their child. The child floundered in the water, over there." She pointed toward the ocean. "Hanalei's great-grandmother swam out to the child and pulled her to the beach where she breathed life back into her."

"What an interesting way to acquire land." James commented.

"Yes. The girl's mother owned many pieces of land, and she wanted her gift to honor the place where her daughter received the breath of life, the *mauli ola*."

James glanced at Hoku. She stared into the distance, as though she could see back in time. "That's a beautiful story, Roselani."

"We married right here in the spot Hawaiians say is sacred. Our wedding gift from Hanalei's grandmother was the title to this land with the agreement that we honor his great-grandmother's desire to share the Hawaiian culture and spread aloha."

James began to understand the family's attachment to the property. He calculated the advantage of a family so attached to the land they would agree to most anything to keep it.

"Anyway," Roselani continued, "my husband saved his money while in the military and borrowed a little more to build the first section of the Breezeway. Just as we do now, we used the luau grounds to host cultural events. The bandstand, dressing room, and stage were added about twenty years ago."

Roselani pointed to the main building. "We had only five suites to start. Enough room to house five families, including our own. Would you like to see my suite?"

As they walked around, James knew Sam took notes on possible maintenance issues—broken tiles, outdated fixtures, the condition of the furnishings, and the age of the appliances. And as much as James enjoyed Roselani's stories of the old days, he mentally took notes about all the changes he expected to make when he became manager. There was no doubt in his mind that he would acquire this property.

After they'd inspected the kitchen, *lū'au* grounds, swimming pool, walkways, and four of the twenty suites, James felt ready to negotiate his final offer. "Thank you, Roselani for sharing the rich history of this place."

James turned to Kawika. "Is your family prepared to continue negotiations?"

Hoku spoke for the first time on the tour. "Before we continue negotiations, my family thought you both might like to see the south end of our island and the Volcanoes National Park."

"Will you be our guide on this tour, as well?" James asked Roselani.

"I will," Hoku said.

****

Two hours later, Hoku met James in the lobby. "Aloha," she greeted him. "Is Mr. Sagal joining us?"

"I convinced Sam to stay behind and work on business."

Hoku couldn't stop the smile that crept across her face. It was a long trip. She would have James to herself for the rest of the day and into the night.

"How far away is this volcano?" James asked.

"Two hours."

"Shall we get started?" he asked.

"Wait," Hoku said as she looked over his shoulder at the sketch he held in his hands. "Is that our lobby?"

"Yes. It's just an idea of how to renovate if we reach a satisfactory agreement."

She looked at the sketch and pointed to something in the middle of the room. "May I ask what this is?" She scrunched up her brow and cocked her head.

James laid the sketch down on a table. "I'm not much of an artist, but picture a black lacquer table with a three-foot tall vase of tropical flowers. Maybe a red vase with those flowers that are shaped like this." James held his wrist at a ninety-degree angle to his arm. "And they have those red flower parts that stick up."

"Do you mean birds-of-paradise?"

"Yes, I think that's the name. Wouldn't that grab your attention?"

"Birds-of-paradise are a lovely flower, but…"

"But, what?"

"Maybe it's the location of the table and vase that I can't picture. Besides, when you enter the lobby now, what do you see?"

"Brown-tones. Hieroglyphics."

Hoku laughed. "The hieroglyphics are replicas of petroglyphs from the sixteenth century. The muted tones of the lobby allow the natural beauty of the outside to dominate." She turned his body so he faced the ocean. "Now what do you see?"

James looked beyond the open-air lobby to the outdoor spaces. "I see palm trees, sand, ocean."

"Now that grabs your attention!"

"Okay. Well, it's just an idea." He wadded up the piece of paper and tossed it into the waste bin. "Let's agree to ban any conversations about business for the rest of today. I just want to enjoy the scenery and get to know you better."

Hoku replied. "You won't be disappointed."

****

James listened while Hoku talked almost non-stop about what they saw as they drove south on Highway 11 past coffee farms and into the lava flows of the Ka`u district. "Pele was not pleased with the occupants, so she sent the burning lava across their land."

"Pele?"

"Yes, the Goddess of the Volcano erupts when angered by something or somebody. I've packed a traditional gift, a *ho'okupu*, for her, but she also likes an occasional cigar."

"Your goddess likes cigars?"

"She can connect with the ashes that they form."

They stopped at the small village of Volcano to eat lunch before they entered the national park. Hoku took James to her favorite Thai restaurant and they shared conversation about the climate of the different parts of the island. "I'm glad you recommended I bring a jacket," James commented. "The mist makes it cool up here, doesn't it?"

"I always travel with five things: a water bottle, jacket, change of clothes, hiking boots, and a swimsuit. That way, I'm prepared for some exercise and the comfort of driving home in clean, dry clothes."

James appreciated a woman who planned. It was a great trait for business, but admitted to himself that he preferred spontaneity when it came to personal relationships.

Hoku pulled into a parking area near the edge of a steaming crater. James gathered up his water bottle and jacket and followed her to the rim of the crater where he could see a collection of what looked like trash, scattered along the edges.

"Offerings." Hoku said simply as she pointed to the various bottles of alcohol and flowers. "Shall I try to appease Pele with a chant?"

"How does she behave when she's appeased?"

"She will quiet herself, sometimes for years, until she feels threatened or upset again."

"What should I do?"

"Close your eyes and feel her presence."

James closed his eyes and felt the breeze brush across his face and the sting of sulfur in his nostrils. He heard Hoku calling to the Goddess Pele. The huskiness of her singing voice surprised and soothed him. With each repetition of the haunting verse, Hoku's voice grew stronger. James didn't open his eyes until she fell silent for several seconds. He watched as Hoku laid the ceremonial gift on the side of the crater.

James felt so unbelievably altered by her. He was a player, not a man who settled for one woman. And yet, at that moment, he could not imagine himself with any other woman for the rest of his life.

Hoku reached her arms forward, hand over hand and bowed her head. Then, as if in a trance, she muttered something. James tracked her every movement as she approached him.

"Did you feel her?" she asked.

"I felt many things." He gently touched her cheek with the back of his hand. "You are so incredibly beautiful." James wanted to kiss her, to hold her in his arms and make promises he could keep, but he wanted to do it right. He needed to be sure that she wanted him as much as he wanted her. He looked into her eyes and saw his future.

****

Hoku held her breath when James touched her cheek. She wanted the moment to last, but couldn't encourage him. She reached for his hand and led him to the car.

Hoku planned to keep their relationship professional. Her allegiance must be to her family. Why, then, did she beg Pele to help her build a life with James?

If only I hadn't promised Kawika, she thought.

The sun started to dip below Mauna Loa as Hoku drove down Chain of Craters Road. James laid his hand on top of hers on the gearshift and squeezed. She felt a longing between her legs and her nipples hardened. Like Pele awakening from a long rest, Hoku felt the heat rise in her core.

By the time they parked the car and started the trek across the lava fields, Hoku told herself she was thankful that the uneven terrain and the necessity to hold a flashlight made it difficult to hold hands. She insisted on leading the way so she could pay attention to her footing and not think too much about James and his lean body, reassuring hands, and alluring dimple.

Heat rose from the stark lava as they got closer to the active flow. Near the end of the trail, they could hear the hissing sound of liquid rock as it contacted the water. They stopped to marvel at the wonder of molten lava flowing into the ocean. James placed his arm around Hoku's waist. "I think I've been transformed tonight."

She allowed herself to lean into his body. "So have I," she admitted.

James embraced her, both hands moving slowly up and down the small of her back and drawing her closer until she lifted her chin to accept his eager kiss. Forgetting where she was and why she was here, Hoku wrapped her arms around his neck and parted her lips to relish the feel of his tongue on hers. His hands cupped her rear and pulled her even closer.

Suddenly, she jerked away and grabbed his hands. He leveraged his strength to pull her back. Her breasts were once more touching his chest and his mouth went to her neck.

"Hoku, don't pull away," he begged.

"I can't. We can't. Not here. It's disrespectful."

"Where then? When?"

Hoku crimped her lips and gathered her strength before she pushed her body away from James once again. This was not the place and this could not be the man. She promised Kawika she would stay away from James.

She forced the words from her mouth. "There are many sacred places in Hawai'i. This is one of my favorites, and I'm glad I could share it with you. I think we both know that we can't think of this trip as anything more than the sharing of a cultural experience."

"Hoku, listen—"

She placed her fingers on his lips. "Shh. What we've shared here is special. Please leave it at that."

Chapter Four

Early the next morning, the ring of Hoku's cell phone interrupted a delicious dream about James.

"Well?"

"Kawika? Is that you?" Hoku yawned.

"Of course, it's me. Who did you expect?"

"I don't know. I'm not really awake yet."

"Late night?"

"Yes."

"Is he still there?"

"No. He's not here. But I must say I wouldn't mind if he was."

"And why didn't Sagal go with you two? The plan was to take both men."

"How did you know?"

"I have my sources."

"James said Sam stayed behind to get some work done," she said in her own defense.

"So James could be alone with you. How convenient."

Hoku thought, *More than convenient. It was amazing.*

"Hoku?"

"What?"

"How can you help make a business decision if you get involved with Westerman?"

"I didn't get involved with him. I thought you agreed I should take him to the volcano."

"Yeah, well now I'm not so sure."

"Enough, Kawika. We don't have anything to fear from James. He only wants to help us."

"How long have you run your own business, Hoku? You and I both know James is here to make money—pure and simple. He'll promise you the moon right now to get your agreement on his offer."

"I'm not asking for the moon, but honestly, I'd like another chance at love. Don't you want that for yourself, Kawika?"

"You know how I feel about replacing Janice. I'm done with love."

"I thought I was. Now I don't know."

"For God's sake, James Westerman is just a man. If you want to fall in love, choose a guy from the island who won't desert you."

"James is not Martin. You're not giving him a fair chance."

"I'm sorry, but he *is* from the mainland, and you don't even know if he'll stay here. You, of all people, should know how that goes. How many times have we seen people come from the mainland and not acclimate to Hawai'i?"

"And just as many, or more, do make it here."

"More importantly, we're in negotiations with him. There are plenty of other men, Hoku."

"Look, I didn't do anything except show him the south end of the island and Volcano Park," she lied.

"Keep it that way, okay?"

"I'll see you later." She hung up.

She didn't even recognize herself anymore. When did she start lying to her family? She promised Kawika she'd stay away from James, and last night on the lava field, she broke that promise.

Kawika might be right. Hadn't she trusted Martin and let his lust for her cloud her judgment? Look where that got her—two weeks from the altar before she discovered what kind of man Martin was.

But, what if Kawika was wrong? What if James was the perfect match for her? He wasn't anything like Martin. James listened to her when she talked. He made her laugh with his jokes, and he was interested in the culture. Not once did Martin accompany her to pay tribute to the Goddess Pele or view the lava flow. Last night when James held her in his arms and kissed her, she felt as though he was a man she could trust. A man she could even love.

She shook herself. What was she thinking? Hadn't a mainlander already scorned her? How could she trust that James wasn't just trying to sleep with her?

Hoku needed to forget about the way James admitted he wanted her. She needed to forget about the way his hands and lips aroused a long dormant heat in her. And, she especially needed to extinguish any notion of falling in love with him.

She poured her second cup of coffee and the phone rang again. Her mom relayed the message that James's brother was in town for a couple of days and James called to invite them for a sunset sail that evening.

"I have to do my show, Mom," Hoku said.

"I already phoned Puahi to see if she could cover your dinner show and she can."

"I don't know if I want to go, Mom."

"Nonsense. We should all go. You know, James's brother might be the person who will manage the Breezeway if we make a deal. We should get to know him."

Hoku slumped into a kitchen chair, bumped her coffee cup and spilled the hot brew into her lap. *Great. What else could go wrong?* It hadn't occurred to her that someone else may stay on as manager if the two families reached an agreement.

"Hokulani?" Her mom's voice interrupted her thoughts. "Are you okay?"

"Yeah, I spilled my coffee."

"I will see you at the harbor later today."

Hoku grabbed a dishcloth to wipe up the mess. Did she want James to stay? She just didn't know anymore. She needed time to think it through. The only thing that seemed certain was how she felt when James touched her.

She called her Mom back and asked her to fill in if anyone signed up for the cultural class. Hoku spent the day at home in preparation for the sail. She changed her clothes several times before she settled on a V-necked blue and green floral sundress, blue shrug, and green sandals. She brushed her hair and pulled one side back behind her ear and attached three white gardenias. After one last look in the mirror, she grabbed her bag and locked the house.

Kawika and Roselani were already at *Honokohau* Harbor when she arrived. James made introductions and ushered everyone onto the fifty-foot sloop. When he held her hand to help her aboard, she squeezed and held on longer than necessary. He placed his hand on the small of her back to guide her into the cabin, and she very nearly came undone.

They sat in the spacious interior seating area and David poured glasses of champagne. "May we each get what we most desire," he said as he raised his glass.

I won't get everything I desire if James goes back to the mainland, Hoku thought.

They set sail and headed north past the airport and the first of the large resorts. The calm water helped to sooth her nerves. David waved in the general direction of the first resort and said, "Ah, the big boys. Playground for the stars."

James quipped, "It's not how big you are. It's about the bottom line." He raised his glass. "Here's to a better bottom line. Cheers."

Roselani proposed an additional toast. "To our *'ohana*." The group raised their glasses again.

David asked, "What does that mean?"

"Family," James answered.

"How did you know that?" Hoku asked.

"The emcee at the luau."

Again, Hoku noted James was an excellent listener—a trait Martin lacked.

Roselani did most of the talking for the Kawelu clan. She shared stories of the early days of Kona and how she and Hanalei advertised to get their first guests.

"We thought, why not send invitations to everyone we knew? We asked our business associates to recommend us to their clients and for our friends to bring their families to the luau. I handwrote over two hundred invitations and included coupons for free drinks and breakfast with a one-night stay and a third night free when guests paid for two nights. We promised the best hospitality, stunning ocean view rooms and free entertainment and cultural classes. Within six months we were booked to full capacity over ninety percent of the time." She laughed. "Of course, we only had four suites back then, plus ours."

"Do all of the suites still have ocean views?" David asked.

"Yes. And they are all the same price. We do not have full ocean view, partial ocean view, terrace, or view of the rooftop like some of the 'big boys,' as you call them."

Hoku admired the way her mom made people feel comfortable and encouraged them to talk and laugh, and it didn't escape her that James and David were both attentive to her mom's stories.

"David," Roselani asked, "how long will you stay on the island?"

"Oh, just a day or two. I need to get back to Colorado to sign the agreement before I jump into management mode there."

David's not here to manage. Hoku drew in a big breath of air and exhaled. *That must mean James will stay.* She covered her smile with her hand.

"Kawika, what is your favorite memory of growing up at the Breezeway?" James asked.

Kawika was silent for a moment, then answered, "The day I met Janice. She was travelling with her family from Oahu. I was home from college for the summer, and she just graduated from high school. We were married by the end of the summer."

"Ah," David said, "love at first sight. Why didn't she come?"

Hoku murmured, "She passed away eight years ago." She reached across the table and took her brother's hand.

"I'm so sorry, Kawika," David said.

"Me, too." Kawika looked away.

"And your favorite memory, Hoku?" James prompted.

"There are so many, but I'll tell you about my grandmother." Hoku thought for a few seconds. "My *tūtū* used to sit with Dad on the lanai and make ti leaf leis for our guests. I loved to listen to her tell stories of our

Hawaiian gods and goddesses. I imagined she was a goddess when the trade winds blew her hair away from her face.

"*Tūtū* taught me my first hula dance and how to carve out a gourd to make an implement we call an *ipu*."

"She sounds wonderful," James said.

"She was. I mean, she is," Hoku answered. "She's with me every day."

"My brother tells me it's a transformational experience to watch you dance," David said.

"Transformational?" Kawika shot a warning look at Hoku.

James cleared his throat. "Maybe Hoku would do a private show for us now."

"I don't have my music."

"I can sing," Roselani volunteered. She stood up and started to hum a tune and tap her foot. "How about, "Little Grass Shack"?" Leave it to Roselani to lighten the mood.

"All right." Hoku took off her sandals and positioned herself in front of the brothers.

Roselani sang, and Hoku easily performed the familiar movements.

Hoku liked the way the brothers stared at her—especially James. The *'a'ama* movement was very effective when her rayon skirt licked her knees as she shimmied sideways, like a crab, with her heels lifted from the floor. When she finished, James and David clapped and whistled while Kawika just sipped his drink.

Hoku dabbed a tissue at droplets of perspiration between her breasts and excused herself to the deck to cool off. She heard the door open and close to the cabin, and guessed it was James even before she turned to see him.

"Thank you for dancing," he said.

"My pleasure."

He stepped to the rail and stood beside her. "About last night. I am transformed—and baffled. I don't usually feel this way about women."

She stifled the smile that tugged at the corners of her mouth. "And I feel something for you, too." She felt James's hand at the small of her back and shivered at his touch. "I can't, James. I won't let myself fall for a mainlander again."

"But I want to be an islander. If our families make a deal, I'm here for at least three years—longer if it works out."

"If what works out?"

"Us," he said. "Do we have a chance?"

She could no longer deny her feelings. Kawika had no right to control her by extracting promises from her. She was a grown woman and could decide for herself if a mainlander was right for her. She stood on her tiptoes and whispered in his ear. "We have a chance."

James took her hand and led her around the starboard side of the boat where no one could see them. He wrapped his arms around her, and pulled her body to his.

Hoku lifted her chin and felt his mouth capture hers. She opened her lips for his probing tongue and shivered as their tongues danced between their mouths. Her back arched, and she moaned as he kissed his way down her neckline.

She pulled away at the sound of footsteps.

"Celebrating in private?" It was David.

Hoku slowed her breathing, smoothed down her dress, and straightened her hair. "I was just going back in." She started to walk away.

"Wait." James reached for her hand and pressed his room key into it.

Hoku bit her bottom lip and slipped the key into her bra. The feel of the metal against her breast made her anxious for things she wanted—a husband and a family of her own.

Hoku wondered if James wanted the same things she did. He alluded to a relationship when they were at the crater's edge and again on the deck tonight. Was he the one she had been waiting for?

Hoku hummed her favorite Hawaiian love song as she drove from the pier to the Breezeway. She parked among the guests' cars and used a back entrance to avoid the front lobby.

She climbed the stairs to the second floor and started down the corridor toward her destiny, the precious key grasped tightly in her hand. She stopped outside James's door when she heard David's voice. She couldn't very well let herself in with David in the room, so she just stood there for a moment trying to decide what to do. She tried not to eavesdrop, but when she heard her name mentioned, she couldn't help herself.

"So, would you get out of here? I'm supposed to meet Hoku."

"Ah," David said, "the newest distraction before Marta even returns from her buying trip. I have every confidence you'll lose to me again this round of competition."

Marta? Competition? The words pounded at her temples.

"Marta and I have a mutual understanding—you know, friends with benefits. Nothing more. And the reason I haven't won the last two rounds is because I've been too soft. I can see that now. So look out. I'll be laughing all the way to the bank with Father's prize money."

Hoku bit her fist as she made her way back down the stairs to the kitchen service door. When she saw Tatiana, she let the tears flow.

"How could I be so stupid?"

"What happened?" Tatiana rubbed her shoulders and walked her back out the kitchen door to the lawn.

"It's James."

"The investor? When I talked to you on the phone, I thought you said things were going well."

"He gave me the key to his room. I'm so stupid. I planned to use it." Hoku covered her face with her hands and shook her head.

"I don't understand," Tatiana said.

"I thought he was interested in me. It turns out his investment in the Breezeway is just part of some rich boys' contest."

"Did he tell you that? I still don't understand."

"No, he failed to tell me the real reason he wants to invest in the Breezeway. He used me so my family would agree to bring him in, and now he's pretending to be interested in me. It's Martin all over again."

"If James didn't tell you about this, how do you know?"

"I overheard him talking to his brother."

"Maybe you misunderstood."

"I always misunderstand. What is it with men and me? I didn't get it with Martin and I don't get it with James."

"I'm sorry, Hoku. But don't be so hard on yourself. At least you found out about James early on."

"I'm done with men. I hate to admit it, but Kawika was right."

"About what?"

"He warned me about getting interested in another mainlander. He's right that mainlanders don't always stay in Hawai'i. That they don't get our culture. That it's just not a good fit for me."

"Kawika is a bitter widower, Hoku. All men are not like Martin and James. Look at my Nathan. He came from Michigan, and he loved Hawai'i."

"Your Nathan was special, Tatiana." Hoku felt guilty about having a pity party in front of Tatiana who lost her husband to cancer. "I'm sorry. I shouldn't whine about this to you after all you've been through."

Tatiana wiped a tear from her face. "I miss Nathan, but I'm thankful every day that he was in my life, and that we had a son together. The perfect man will come along when you least expect it. I have faith that you will find someone."

"I don't. And now, if we reach an agreement, it looks as though James may be here for three years. At least Martin left the island."

"I wish it'd worked out, Hoku. I really want you to be happy."

"Me, too. The other day when I took James to the crater, I actually started to believe that I could be married and start a family." She started to sob again. "I don't want to be by myself forever."

Chapter Five

James opened his eyes and groaned when he remembered that Hoku didn't show up the night before. He had never been around anyone as fickle as her. He planned to force her hand today. No more cat and mouse games for him.

He showered and dressed, then picked up the phone to call the Kawelu family back into negotiations. David's deal was completed and if James couldn't come to an agreement in the next couple of days, he'd have to face his father's chastisement, and worse, settle for an investment near Boston.

James waited for Hoku in the hallway outside of Roselani's office. He deserved an explanation.

"Hoku?" he called to her when he saw her approach.

"James." She reached for the door handle of her mom's office.

"A word, please," he said.

Hoku dropped her hand to her side and marched down the hallway.

"I waited for you until two in the morning," James said.

"Keep your voice down," she scolded as she spun on her heels to face him. "I changed my mind."

"You could have called."

Hoku looked up at him, hands on her hips. "I don't appreciate being used as a pawn. Is the Breezeway nothing more than a competition between two spoiled rich boys who have nothing better to do than play with their money?"

"What are you talking—?"

"I heard you and David talking last night."

"So you did come." James raised his eyebrows and grinned at her.

"You arrogant bastard."

"I can explain."

"Explain away, James. How dare you think I'm someone who just sleeps around. I'm not willing to be friends with benefits, like this Marta woman. I wouldn't even call you a friend at this point."

"Are you ready to listen?"

"No. I don't think so. I can't believe you. I know you are investing to turn a profit, but if you are basing your decisions on beating your brother at some testosterone-based pissing match, then I don't trust you. The Breezeway is not your playground, James, it's my family home."

"I never referred to you as a friend with benefits. I've been honest with you about my intentions. I want us to have a relationship."

"Well, that's not going to happen. I plan to keep as far away from you as possible."

James snickered. "Is that so? I usually get what I want, Hula Hips, and I want you. I'll find a way to keep you close until you see I'm one of the good guys."

She reached in her purse, took out his room key and shoved it at him. "This is one time you won't get what you want."

James followed her back down the hallway. When they entered her mom's office, Kawika's stare did not escape James.

"Bottom line," James said as soon as he opened his briefcase. "I think we agree on several points including the itemized list of needed maintenance and renovations for the dining room, the five oldest suites and the lobby."

There, he thought, *they are nodding.*

"A computer system is non-negotiable. The cost of equipment and the installation would increase our holdings another quarter percent or so."

Kawika responded, "We're willing to increase the amount of your equity, but not especially for a computer system that we don't feel we need."

"But you do need a computer system. The accounting system we use for the Westerman properties is computerized. And the security of your guests is at risk. With key cards, codes change with every guest, so they know they are secure in their suites." James held up the key Hoku handed to him just minutes before. "Honestly, as charming as this is, it's a security risk.

"At any rate," James continued, "if we come to an agreement, we will insist on a computer system."

"I see," Kawika said.

James and Kawika glared at one another for several seconds before Kawika continued. "Are you willing to have a conversation about the management of the Breezeway?"

"I'd like to hear what your family thinks," James answered.

"What we offer is expertise in running a service industry in Hawai'i. Our specialty is service, and while we weren't as strong with the financial side of the business, the service we offer is what brings people back to the Breezeway," Kawika said.

"I'm not sure what your point is," James said.

"We understand that the Westerman Corporation typically takes over management as part of your investment model. We think you have a lot to gain by deviating from that model for this property. Co-management would cover both bases of strong financial governance and local Hawaiian service and cultural experiences for our guests."

James rubbed his chin with his right hand. While he negotiated, it was his habit to make the business owners squirm a bit before he agreed to one of their demands. Kawika was his target, but when he saw Hoku fidget in her chair, her delicious lips quivering, he had an idea. "If you agree to sign over twenty-five percent of your holdings, I'll agree to joint management with the condition that I choose the co-manager."

Sam laid his hand on James's arm. "Could I see you in the hallway?"

"Excuse us." James followed Sam out the door.

"Are you kidding me? Your father will have your neck. I told you from the start not to let a woman get in the way of business."

"Relax, Sam. You know me better than that. I'm agreeing to joint management to placate this family because I can see potential in the property. Hell, the land alone is a gold mine. Do you honestly think I will lose control of management? Listen and learn." He reached for the doorknob and straightened his shoulders before he re-entered the office.

As soon as they walked in the door, James announced, "I'll agree to joint management on the condition that Hoku is the co-manager."

"What about Mom?" Hoku blurted out.

"I don't really want to manage anymore, Hokulani. Maybe James will keep me on part-time as hostess or greeter in the lobby," Roselani said.

James nodded. "If that's what you'd like, Mrs. Kawelu, we can work that out."

"Kawika? Will you support your sister in the co-manager position?"

"Of course I'll support her. I don't like the way you're doing this, Westerman, but I'll support her."

"You can think about it, but those are my final terms. I expect to hear from you in twenty-four hours."

****

"What the hell, Hoku?" Kawika bellowed, as soon as James and Sam left the office.

"I didn't have any idea he would do that. You have to believe me."

"Hoku is the logical choice for the position, Kawika. You do not want to manage, and I was in the management position when we fell behind in our obligations. She is a fine choice. You should feel proud of her."

"That'd be easier if I trusted Westerman with my sister."

"Hokulani has to find her own way, Kawika."

"What choice do we have?" Hoku asked. "If we don't agree to James's proposal, we'll lose the Breezeway for sure."

"That's the worst of it. We don't have any other options, so I guess Westerman gets what he wants."

Not everything he wants, Hoku thought. *He doesn't get me.*

"I'll call him tomorrow," Kawika said. "He can wait one more night for an answer."

The next morning, Hoku awoke with a new resolve to keep her relationship with James professional, especially now that she was the co-manager. She couldn't understand why she felt so attracted to him anyway. He was just a man, as Kawika so clearly pointed out, who came to town to make some money and have some fun. In any case, he already had a woman. Marta. Wasn't that her name? Well, James could just wait for Marta to come around.

Hoku knew she wanted more than a casual relationship. She craved what her parents had—a close, respectful, fun relationship. James was no better than Martin.

Why couldn't she pick a man she could rely on? She'd trusted Martin and believed he would make decisions that were good for both of them, and yet, he insisted they move to the mainland. He went to California and looked for a job and a house. At least, that's what he told her. And she believed him because she wanted to, needed to. He said she needed to be in Kona to finalize the wedding plans. When he returned, he showed her photos of the house he'd bought with a down payment from her parents.

Martin went back to his position at the Breezeway as assistant manager, a post her dad offered him as temporary employment until the move. Hoku stayed busy making plans for the wedding, teaching her classes, and performing five nights a week at the Breezeway. She had even started to pack away her things in anticipation of the move to California. As much as she wanted to stay in Hawai'i, she'd trusted that Martin chose a place for them to live that would be beneficial for them both. Besides, they planned to start a family as soon as they settled into the new house, and Hoku would be busy preparing for the little one. She planned to offer some ukulele and hula classes at the local YMCA as a way to spread the Hawaiian culture in California. She thought she'd done a great job of convincing herself she would love this new place because she would be with the one she loved.

Hoku poured herself a second cup of coffee and wiped her eyes with the back of her hand. She traced the pattern of the orchids on the tablecloth that graced the table on her lanai. The tablecloth reminded her of the late night dinners Martin and she shared after she got home from her evening performances. They sat on the lanai and looked out over the coffee orchards into the moonlit Pacific Ocean. She served a simple meal that she'd prepared earlier in the day, and Martin selected a bottle of wine. In those days, he couldn't keep his hands off her. They barely finished eating before his hand found her thigh and his lips nibbled at her ears. They rarely made it inside the house before the lovemaking began. Hoku relished the privacy her little house on the hill provided. She could have stayed with Martin on that lanai forever and lived on love.

And then, everything changed.

Hoku repeatedly came home to an empty house and believed Martin's excuses about getting hung up with his golf partners at a bar or losing track of the time at a dinner meeting. She noticed he smelled of alcohol and heavy cologne and that his clothes were rumpled. She noticed, but ignored the signs. Hoku went on believing his lies because when he entered the bedroom and lay beside her, he called her his only love and promised their babies would be the most beautiful children in the world. She opened her arms and legs for him and pretended it was all true.

And then one night, he neglected to come home at all. When he showed up after eight in the morning, she wanted to believe him when he said he left the bar and thought he would just take a nap before he drove home, and he'd slept all night in the parking lot.

"Which parking lot?" she asked.

She would never forget his icy glare. "What do you mean 'which parking lot?' I came home, didn't I?"

He frightened her, so she dropped it. "I'm sorry you had to sleep in the car. Are you hungry?"

He picked her up then, and carried her to their bedroom where he kissed her as he frantically removed her clothes. "Hungry for you, and only you."

She thought about how he would carry her that way when they entered their honeymoon suite and that he deserved to have some time with his buddies at the bar before the wedding. After all, she would have him for the rest of their lives.

And then he stayed out another night, and another and Hoku confided in Tatiana that she feared he was having an affair. Hoku decided to follow him after work as he drove the forty miles to Waimea and parked in front of a palatial house. She drove by the house three nights in a row, and then asked Tatiana to come with her while she confronted him.

Hoku asked Tatiana to wait in the car. Her legs felt like they might collapse and the bile in the back of her throat burned as she knocked on the door and called his name. When there was no immediate answer, rage took over and both fists pounded on the door as she shouted, "Answer the door, you coward."

A woman opened the door, dressed only in Martin's aloha shirt. "What do you want?"

Hoku yelled. "Go to hell, you bastard." She jerked off her engagement ring and threw it across the floor.

The woman at the door called over her shoulder. "Martin, baby, you naughty boy. You didn't tell me you had a fiancée."

Martin called from another room. "I have everything I need right here."

The woman threw her head back and laughed before she closed the door.

It was the only time in her life that Hoku drank until she got drunk. And as painful as it had been, she finally felt that she could move forward. She just needed to find the right man.

Hoku wished she could go back and change the past, but all she could do was move forward and hope for the best.

That evening, Hoku sat at her vanity in the dressing room preparing for her performance. A knock on the door sent the girls into a tizzy. "Get the door, Lei," Hoku said.

Her niece opened the door and let out a squeal. "Who are those for?"

"Hokulani Kawelu."

"I'll give them to her." Lei took the flowers and the envelope.

"Lei," Hokulani called and handed her niece two dollars. "Tip the courier."

Hoku ripped open the envelope and read the congratulatory letter printed on Westerman Corporation letterhead.

Lei smelled the flowers and looked over Hoku's shoulder. "Look what Auntie got from James somebody."

"Why didn't you tell us you have a boyfriend?" one of the dancers teased.

"He's not my boyfriend. He's our new partner."

"I wish my boyfriend would send me flowers," Lei said dreamily.

"What boyfriend?" Hoku's ears perked up. Lei didn't usually keep things from her. "Let's step out for a few minutes."

Hoku stood directly in front of her niece. "Why haven't you mentioned him, Lei?"

"Because Dad told me I couldn't date him."

"Oh, Lei. Is this the twenty-four-year-old?"

Hoku's niece pouted and swirled her foot around in the grass. "He loves me. And I love him."

"He's told you this already? That he loves you?"

"He's nicer to me than any other guy I've ever known. I'm tired of boys my age. Roland is so much more mature."

"Are you sleeping with him?"

"Auntie!"

"Well. Are you?"

"I love him, so it's okay, right? It's not like I sleep around."

Hoku took her hands. "I didn't mean to imply that you sleep around. I'm not happy that you're having sex at seventeen, but you are. Are you using protection?"

Lei looked down. "It happens so fast. We forget to use anything."

Hoku sighed and held her niece. "May I make an appointment for you to get some birth control?"

"Okay. Sure."

"And will you promise to tell your dad?"

"I'll try."

Hoku could just imagine her brother's reaction to this news. Ever since his wife died eight years ago, she watched her brother struggle to raise a child alone. The night of the car accident, Janice and nine-year-old Lei walked away unscathed after they were broadsided by an SUV. Or so they thought.

Janice and Kawika had Lei thoroughly examined in the emergency room, but Janice refused an exam. The next morning, Kawika slipped out of bed early so Janice could sleep in. At eleven, when he and Lei went to wake her up, Janice was unresponsive. The autopsy indicated that the cause of death was internal bleeding from a ruptured spleen. Kawika never forgave himself for not insisting Janice undergo a complete examination in the emergency room.

At twenty-two, Hoku easily stepped in as the mother figure. Lei shared the same love of hula as Hoku, and Hoku felt that one day her niece would win the title of "Miss Aloha" in the annual Merrie Monarch Hula Competition. Lei focused on this goal for the past two years. Now, with this boyfriend in the picture, Hoku worried that Lei would lose focus and desire for the competition. And for all they'd gone through, Lei never asked Hoku to keep a secret from Kawika.

Chapter Six

Two days later, Hoku sat in her mom's office and signed the papers that made her the co-manager of the Breezeway. Bile collected in the back of her throat as she realized her family also just signed away twenty-five percent of their assets. The onus was on her to protect what was left of the 'āina ho'oilina, their inherited, sacred, land.

Hoku felt her mom's hand on her shoulder. "I'm packing up my personal things today. Is there anything in the office you want me to leave for you?"

"Dad's desk. And the blue bowl." Hoku stared at her hands. "I want to keep flowers in the bowl like you did for Dad." Her chest heaved, and her hands shook. "I don't think I can do this." She sank into her mom's arms.

"You are stronger than you think, Hokulani. You will do what is right."

The next morning, Hoku told herself she just needed to get through the first day at the office with James. Just one day, then another, until the temptation left.

She popped her head into her mom's suite before she faced James. There, in the middle of her mom's living room was her dad's teak desk. "Mom, you should've told me you wanted Dad's desk."

"Oh, I do not want it especially. I left it in the office for you. But then, about an hour ago, Keoni and the boys knocked on my door and said the boss asked if I wanted to keep the teak desk. I assumed you changed your mind."

"That bastard," Hokulani mumbled. "Let me just go see what Mr. Westerman has done with our office."

She marched down the hallway and stormed the office like a tsunami. "What do you think you are doing?"

"Good morning to you, too."

"Why would you take my dad's desk out of here? I planned to use that desk. We left you half the space."

"I ordered two workstations. One for each of us. Equally sized and large enough to accommodate the computer equipment we'll both need."

"Workstations? I don't want a workstation. I want a desk. My dad's desk." Hoku realized she acted like a child. "You had no right to make that decision for me."

"And I had no idea that you would react this way. What is this really about, Hoku? Are you still mad about my family competition?"

"I'm angry that you're already making decisions for me. We're supposed to make decisions together according to the agreement we signed yesterday."

"Like I said, I had no idea you would react this way."

"You could've asked me about the desk."

James smirked. "That's pretty hard to do when you've avoided me and my calls for three days."

Hoku knew he was right. She couldn't have it both ways. She needed to be able to talk to him in order to work with him. Her stomach churned as she realized how difficult this would be.

****

James knew he needed to placate this fiery woman before anything productive could happen. He wished she'd save some of that fire for him outside the office, but reminded himself to bide his time. He'd never failed when it came to winning over a woman, but she was a little more challenging than most.

James contacted Keoni on the walkie-talkie. "Keoni, please bring your crew back up to the office. Ms. Kawelu would like her father's desk brought back."

"What about the workstation?" she sounded like a schoolchild taunting an enemy.

"The desk will work. We'll just have the computer tech punch a couple of holes for the cords."

"Punch holes? In a teak desk? Are you crazy?"

"Or we'll just have cords dangling off the side of your desk. I hear dangling cords are all the rage," he teased.

"No holes."

"Okay. No holes." He would have to placate her further if he was to get any business done today. "Shall we go over our schedule for the week?"

James could practically hear her teeth gnash against one another. "All right."

"I know you need time to teach. What's your current schedule?"

"On Saturdays, I teach my *halau* classes. We also offer a variety of free cultural classes for our guests. If anyone signs up, that's from one to two, Tuesday through Friday. Occasionally, I help Mom organize a special event on the weekends."

"Well then, we'll work around that."

"*Mahalo*."

"I thought we should plan an employee meeting."

She nodded.

James asked her to go over the employee list with him and choose the most experienced person from each department as lead.

He noticed that she actually cracked a smile. "Uncle Dom for the restaurant."

"I didn't know your uncle works here."

"He's not a blood relative, but he's been with my parents from the beginning. 'Uncle' is an endearment."

"Good. Dominidor for the restaurant." James put a check next to his name. "What about the landscaping crew?"

"Keoni. He already organizes the guys, and he has been here the longest of anyone on that crew. He also takes care of the pool maintenance."

Now we're getting somewhere. James noticed Hoku's shoulders relax and her hands calm as they discussed the employees.

After the selection of department leads for all four departments, James proposed the leads keep daily logs and attend weekly planning meetings.

"That seems reasonable," Hoku responded.

"The department leads should be paid a differential for the extra responsibility."

"They'll appreciate that."

They were doing well, so James just kept going. "I thought we could ask the leads to meet with us tomorrow morning and lay out the plan. Say eight? We should establish a regular weekly meeting time."

"How about seven on Tuesdays? That's our slowest morning."

"Sounds good. Would you like to contact the leads about tomorrow's meeting?"

"I'll do that as soon as we're done here," Hoku answered.

"Where shall we hold the meeting?"

"Let's meet at the bandstand on the luau grounds."

James snickered. "The bandstand? Out in the open?"

"It's quiet out there in the mornings."

"Okay, the bandstand then."

Finally, thought James, *we agree on something.*

The next morning, James dressed for the department lead meeting in a short-sleeved, light blue shirt and navy tie. As he approached the bandstand, he spotted Hoku laying a tablecloth over a round banquet table and placing something golden brown in the middle. She'd evidently arrived very early to take control of the environment. James envisioned four chairs facing a podium where he would address the group. He chose not to say anything about the table.

"Good morning," he said.

"Aloha."

James took a seat and removed his papers from his briefcase. Just then, one of the dining room staff appeared with a tray of dishes, pastries and six small bowls of fresh fruit salad. James looked on in disbelief as a waiter delivered a carafe of coffee and pitcher of water. Hoku continued to set the table.

An older-looking man walked tentatively up the walkway.

"Come, Uncle Dom." Hoku walked out to meet him.

James heard her say, "Everything is fine. No, Mom will not be here today." She patted his hand.

James stood and stepped to the side. He wasn't sure why he should sit at the same table with the employees. He motioned for Hoku, but she appeared to be too engaged in greeting and reassuring the employees to see his gesture. After Hoku personally seated the four leads, she began.

"Aloha, and *mahalo* for taking time to meet with us. Before we start, shall we open the gourd, as we open our hearts? Mr. Westerman, please join us."

James started to sit just as everyone else stood. He righted himself as the woman next to him took one hand and Hoku took the other. She chanted in her deep voice and then reached for the gourd in the middle of the table.

"I will begin the *'ōlelo mua*. As I open the gourd we celebrate the opportunity to be together and to make plans for our Breezeway *'ohana*." She lifted a shell filled with sand from inside the gourd and started to slowly pour the sand back into the basket. "I come from Hanalei and Roselani, both one hundred percent Hawaiian. My dad no longer lives on earth. I have one brother, Kawika, and my niece, Lei. I have lived in the Kona district all my life. My purpose on earth is to spread aloha and care for my family." The sand was gone from the shell.

James felt the moisture gather on the palms of his hands. How dare she muddy a business meeting with this cultural mumbo-jumbo. He watched Hoku hand the gourd to Dominidor.

"I come from Ignacio, a laborer in the Philippines, and Alicia, a seamstress. My parents immigrated to Hawai'i during the sugar plantation days and labored in the fields of Ka'u until they passed away. We buried them in Na'alehu Cemetery where we visit them on the first Sunday of every month. My wife, Maricar, is the mother of our two daughters and the blood of my life. My purpose on earth is to care for my family." The sand was gone.

Each employee followed the protocol in this manner until the basket came to James. He cursed Hoku under his breath. He hated to be put on the spot like this. He felt everyone stare at him while he filled the shell.

He stammered, "My-my father's name is Alfred, a descendant of English immigrants, and…um, I don't know about my mother. I have one brother, David, who is two years older. And my purpose is…" He let his voice trail off and quickly poured the remaining sand into the basket.

Hoku took the gourd back and said, "All of our lives are mingled together like these grains of sand. The gourd remains open until the end of our meeting to remind us that we are all shoots of the same taro."

James had no idea what his next move should be.

Hoku invited everyone to enjoy breakfast. She poured coffee and water and they all chatted about one another's families and laughed at anecdotes.

James leaned into Hoku's ear. "I thought we were having a meeting?"

"We are."

"Are we planning to share our plan?"

"After we eat." She went back to patting Uncle Dom's hand and laughing with the rest of them.

The new lead for the housekeeping department tried to engage James in a conversation, but he answered her only briefly about why he was here. Associating with employees in this way was foreign to him, and he felt certain it wasn't a good business practice. The closest he'd ever come to it was the annual picnic, and the Westerman executives sat at a reserved table.

At last, Hoku started the meeting. "You were invited to this meeting because my family wanted you to know about some changes here at the Breezeway." She paused and gave a weak smile.

"Why didn't more people come?" Dom asked.

"Someone had to run the place while we met," she joked. "I recommended your names because you have been with us the longest. How long, Uncle Dom?"

"Thirty-five years."

"And the food only gets better!" Keoni called out.

Look how she coddles them, James thought.

"As you may have heard, my family needed to bring in an investor." The leads mumbled and shifted in their chairs.

"I was selected to co-manage with our new partner, Mr. Westerman."

The group clapped.

"What about Roselani?" Keoni asked.

"She will continue as hostess and greeter. It's what she prefers."

Everyone nodded.

"And now, please show your warmest aloha to our new investor and co-manager of the Breezeway, Mr. James Westerman."

James stood, and Hoku presented him with a black *kukui* nut lei. Her brief hug felt like a tease.

"Thank you. I represent the Westerman Corporation in Boston. After I graduated from Harvard University in Business Administration, I joined my father and brother in the family business. I am here to help make the Kona Breezeway Inn a more profitable company." He paused. The group shifted in their seats again.

"You were invited because Ms. Kawelu and I selected you as leads for your respective departments. You will be our eyes and ears and help us to make the Kona Breezeway Inn as efficient as possible. If any of you are not willing to take on this responsibility, you may make an appointment with me later today to discuss your options."

Everyone squirmed again and gaped at their plates.

Hoku interjected, "You will be paid extra for this responsibility."

James shot her a glance. "It is important for all of us to realize that in order to be a profitable entity we will all need to tighten up some procedures. Ms. Kawelu and I agreed to use checklists of expectations for each department to follow daily, weekly, monthly and yearly." James scanned the faces of the employees and looked for any indications of non-compliance.

"At this point, the Kawelu family and I agree that everyone will retain their positions."

A communal sigh of relief reverberated off the back of the bandstand.

James handed each person a stack of forms for their respective departments. As the employees scanned the forms, he could see their faces change.

"Who fills these out?" Dominidor asked.

"The employees fill in what they did and then you initial. Of course, you initial after you check to see the task is actually completed."

Hoku reached for a copy of the form from the table.

"Why would anyone say they did something if they didn't do it?" Dominidor asked. The others bobbed their heads in agreement.

James tried again. "It is your job as department leads to make sure people do all of their assigned tasks during their shifts as efficiently as possible. The key word is *efficiency*. If you are unable to fulfill the requirements of the position, then, let me reiterate that you should see me privately in my office."

No one spoke as they pored over the evaluations.

Suddenly, Keoni pointed to the bottom of the page. "What does this mean?"

"It means, effective immediately, every employee of the Kona Breezeway Inn is evaluated quarterly and given a score. At the end of the year, if the scores are not high enough, those employees face termination. Department leads will be evaluated by management using similar forms."

Everyone looked away from James toward Dominidor.

Dominidor cleared his throat. "Mr. Westerman, sir, do you think that the employees at the Breezeway do not do their jobs after all of these years?"

James reached for his tie and straightened the knot. "The data we reviewed indicated a long history of good service. It's my vision that in addition to good service, every employee of the Kona Breezeway Inn becomes more efficient so that we can show a greater profit."

James packed his briefcase. "Take a look at the forms and make an appointment to see me if you have further questions or have reservations about your new position."

He hurried up the walkway, satisfied to be back in control.

****

Astounded by James's abrupt departure, Hoku stammered, "I-I'm so sorry, my friends. There has been a misunderstanding. I will speak with Mr. Westerman and sort this out." She excused herself and headed for the office.

When she reached it, Hoku glared at James. "What do you mean *your vision*? Make an appointment with *you*. Talk to *you*. What happened to a united front, James?"

"I apologize. You must understand, I'm not really accustomed to co-managing, let alone socializing with employees."

Hoku refused to raise her voice, but she shook the evaluation forms in his face as she spoke. "And these checklists were not supposed to be evaluation forms. My understanding of our goal was to make sure that tasks are completed in a timely manner. Like, did the dishwasher get all of the dishes washed during his shift?"

"You're making more of this than you need to."

"Don't tell me what I should care about. Do you understand the long relationship and trust we have with these folks? They're my second family." She wished he would pay attention to the nuances of the culture. He seemed interested on the trip to the volcano and when her mom gave the tour. Well, that was then. Past tense.

"You know, you have upset these folks," she tried to calm her voice.

James raked his hand through his hair. "Hoku, we'll never make our profit margin if we coddle the employees. They each have a job to do and I simply expect them to do it."

"Coddle them? Is that what you think my family did all these years? We care about them and they care about us. Relationships matter. You've not only made them feel like they don't do their jobs, you've managed to make them feel like they're not important."

"I'm sure they do their jobs. I'm asking us to take a look at how long it takes to do those jobs. Maybe you're so close to them you don't see what can be improved."

"Money cannot always be the deciding factor, James."

"Really?" He scratched his ear and shook his head. "May I remind you that without the big chunk of money supplied by Westerman Corporation, you'd be kissing this place goodbye?"

"What do you want from me? Should I prostrate myself at your feet to thank you for investing in the Breezeway?"

"I'd like to see that." James snickered.

The door echoed her defiance as it slammed shut behind her.

Chapter Seven

Hoku made her way to the cultural center before she threw a full-blown tantrum. How could she make this work? She stomped her feet and shook her head. How could she face James every day and get anything done? She knew she needed to return to the office and act more professional, but damn it, James went behind her back and circulated evaluation forms that she hadn't approved. How could they get anything done? She needed to appeal to his sense of justice. After all, they had an agreement in writing.

She didn't return to the office until almost eleven. When she entered, James looked up from his new workstation and gave her a quizzical look.

"Can we at least consider throwing out the forms?" Hoku began.

"Can we at least give the forms a chance?" James asked. "How about three months? We'll look pretty ineffectual if we introduce a procedure in the morning and discard it before the end of the day."

Hoku sucked in a deep breath. "All right. All right. Three months. But if anyone wants to make an appointment to meet, you and I must meet with them together."

"Agreed."

She started to tidy up her already neat desk.

"I scheduled the computer technician to meet us at eight tomorrow morning. Does that work for you?" James asked.

"Yes." Hoku knew she sounded curt.

"Hoku? Could we start over? Will you try to trust my judgment about business management? The Westerman Corporation uses these evaluation forms all over the country with remarkable success."

"I want to trust you. I'm just not sure I can."

"What would make you trust me?" James asked. "If we are to manage the inn with any success at all, we will need to trust one another, don't you think?" He looked at her with that impish grin of his.

"I agree we need to trust each other, but I think that comes from respecting the other person's opinion and not doing things behind the other's back. I don't feel that you've done that so far."

James sucked in his lips and closed his eyes. "I'm sorry I upset you with the evaluation forms."

She wanted to believe him, needed to believe him. "Please just realize that one of our successes at the Breezeway is our loyal employee base. I'll try to smooth things over if you promise to include me in any decisions that concern employees. They trust me. It will take them a while to trust you."

"Okay. Now, could we try to prioritize our projects? I'd like the chance to show you what a good guy I can be." James cocked his head.

"I'd like that."

It was easy to agree meeting with the new accountant was a high priority. The Kawelu family already approved the decision that the Westerman Corporation would retain the accounting firm they'd worked with for years. James made a teleconference appointment for later that week. It was not so easy to agree on the timeline for the roof replacement. Hoku wanted the work done in January because that was the lowest occupancy month. James argued that if they waited too long, the roof could begin to leak into the guest rooms. She finally had to agree with his logic. James even suggested that she get the bids from three contractors because she knew the reputations of the local companies.

Her family always hired Ortega Contracting, but Hoku could go along with the request to look at three bids. James said he had a template for contracted work and that they could fill it out together.

She declined his offer. "You fill it out and I'll look it over before we send the work out for bids."

"Are you sure?"

"Like you said, we have to trust one another."

"One more thing," James said. "I'd like your agreement to bring in someone from the Westerman Design Team to sketch ideas for the lobby and dining room renovations. I'll make sure they talk to you and get your input before anything is decided."

"How much will that cost?"

"The corporation covers their salaries. The Breezeway pays for the materials and the installations."

"In that case, I see no reason to delay the process."

James looked at his watch. "It's almost time for your class prep and I have an appointment at two-thirty at that gym on Palani Street. Do you know anything about that place?"

She grinned. "It attracts men who want to buff up and women who are looking for a man."

"Do you go there?" he teased.

"I'm not looking for a man."

"Well, that's good to hear." James winked at her. "I'll be back later for dinner and your show. I've invited an acquaintance to join me for dinner."

Male or female? Hoku wondered. "Don't feel that you need to watch the show every time." Then something occurred to her that made her back stiffen. "Unless the dancers are being evaluated, too?"

James laid his hand on her shoulder and pressed down with a gentleness that oozed honesty. "I go to the show to watch you dance. No ulterior motives."

She wanted to rest her head on his chest and forget about the evaluations and his competition with David. She wanted to start from scratch and allow herself to feel what she felt at the crater's edge and on the deck of the boat. She wanted all of that and more, but she had things to protect—her allegiance to Kawika, the family business and her heart.

Hokulani rushed into the kitchen at three-thirty that afternoon and found one of the housekeepers already helping to cover the kitchen duties. Tatiana was checking the specials for tonight's dinner and guiding the prep work. "How's Uncle Dom?" Hokulani asked as she scrubbed her hands.

"We don't know anything yet. Maricar promised to call as soon as they hear."

"Give me directions. What do you need?"

"If you can direct the prep work, I can finish the soup and the oven entrees. I've never been the main chef, Hoku. I hope I can do it and not disappoint Uncle Dom."

"You can do it. We'll all help."

"I'm glad the ambulance didn't use the siren. I didn't even know they'd been here until I got your call." Hoku grabbed a whole chicken and began to cut it into quarter sections. "What happened, exactly?"

Tatiana told her that she had just begun to cut salmon for the *lomi lomi* when Dominidor fell to his knees in pain. "He just passed out," Tatiana said. "It was so scary. I called 9-1-1 immediately. They asked me if he was breathing. I told them he was. I stayed on the line while I just held Uncle Dom's hand. I guess Thea must have called her mom because Maricar was here before the ambulance arrived. She and Thea went to the hospital. I called you next and then figured out what I could handle as far as the menu. That reminds me, Hoku, have someone pull the menus and slip the substitutions in there. Would you type them up in the office and print copies for me?"

"Anything else?"

"Let me think. We'll need a hostess to replace Maricar and a waitress to replace Thea."

Just then Keoni poked his head in the door. "I heard about Uncle Dom. Need any help?"

"Would you be willing to wait tables?"

That was all it took. Keoni called his wife to bring him a change of clothes and then Hoku sent him to talk to Roselani to see if she could cover for Maricar.

Hoku pulled the menus from the hostess podium and typed the menu options for the night. She asked her mom to put the changed menus inside the menu sleeves.

Another volunteer from the housekeeping staff appeared. "I can take orders," she said. "Hey, Keoni, make sure you keep the guests in water and iced tea. I'll get the alcoholic drinks and food. I think I can remember how to set a table. Better let me do that part."

Keoni saluted her. "Yes, ma'am."

When the receptionist finished her shift, she stopped in to offer help and ask about Dominidor.

"It was his gall bladder," Tatiana explained. "He passed a stone and that's what hurt so much. Maricar called to say Uncle Dom is scheduled for surgery in the morning and then he needs to take a few weeks off work to recuperate. Thank goodness for our medical coverage! His vacation time will cover two of the weeks."

"What can I do to help?"

Tatiana answered, "We're covered for the dinner rush, but we'll need some prep for tomorrow and cleaning help after that. Can you come back about eight?"

Tatiana prepared the barbecue sauce and Hoku chopped vegetables. Lei entered the kitchen. It was obvious that she'd been crying.

"What's the matter, baby?" Hoku put her arms around her little protégé.

"I'm sick again, Auntie. I can't dance tonight and I'm worried about school because Dad won't write me a note to say why I've been absent. I had a fight with him and ran away. I didn't know where to go, so I came to you."

Hoku drew in a big breath as she rubbed the girl's back. Sadly, her brother changed after his wife's death. Kawika was harsh, and said things he didn't mean, but Hoku was sure he'd write the note if she talked to him. "I'll call him, Lei. Take my car and go to my place to rest. I'll call you later." She bit at a hangnail on her finger.

"What's going on?" Tatiana asked.

"Lei's sick again. I need to call Kawika and talk some sense into him about the girl. And, I need to rearrange the show for tonight."

"You guys already know how to do the show without Lei. What's really going on?"

"She ran away. She says Kawika won't write her an absence note for school, but I think it's more than that. I'll check with you later, Tatiana. Right now, I need to call my brother and let him know Lei is safe."

****

James and his guest arrived at the restaurant at James's regular time. Roselani greeted them at the podium with a warm "aloha" and a shell lei.

"And who is this?" Roselani asked.

"Roselani, meet Stanley Caruso. Stanley was my roommate in college."

"Nice to meet you, Stanley. What brings you to Kona?"

"I'm here on business and to check up on this guy," Stanley said and slapped James on the back.

"Welcome, Mr. Caruso."

"Why are you here tonight?" James asked. "I thought it was the other girl's night?"

"Well, with everything that happened around here, when Hokulani sent Keoni to see if I could help out, I jumped at the chance."

Why would Hoku have anything to do with managing the dining staff? Wasn't that why they designated Dominidor?

Roselani led them to James's favorite table and handed them the menus. "May I start you out with a mai tai?"

"Sounds good to me," Stanley said.

James nodded.

"I'll make them myself. Extra cherries and pineapple for your guest, James." Off she went. James was sorry Stanley showed up in town before the renovations. He could just imagine Stanley telling the guys at the Boston Yacht Club that Little Jimmie Westerman bought a hokey little inn that served fruity drinks and he would never learn to run a successful business.

Roselani brought two tall orange tumblers bursting with cherries and pineapple and paper umbrellas. "Welcome to Kona, Stanley. This is the Breezeway's specialty drink. I hope you enjoy it."

James decided to say something to try to save face and show who was boss. "Roselani, I know you are filling in tonight, but maybe we should try to serve our drinks without the umbrellas."

"For goodness sakes. Why? They're so festive!"

"I'm trying to convert the restaurant to a more sophisticated dining experience."

"I see," Roselani said. "Shall I remove the drinks and bring something else?"

"Nonsense," Stanley piped in. "You'd have to pry this drink out of my hands now that I've tasted it. In fact, I'd like another one just like this when you get a chance." He winked at Roselani and she scurried off.

"Thanks for being a good sport, Stanley," James said.

"Not a problem. The hostess seems to like making mai tais and I like drinking them. It's a win-win situation."

Just then, Keoni brought water and greeted them. "Good evening, gentlemen."

"Keoni?" James asked.

"Yes, sir?"

"Since when did you begin moonlighting in the restaurant?"

"Just helping out, sir," Keoni answered. "Hoku told me what to say."

James shook his head and knew he'd have to say something to Hoku about this level of micromanaging. Perhaps she misunderstood the model they'd implemented. He started to recommend the chicken luau when Stanley said, "I think I'll try the barbecued chicken, thanks."

"Sure. I didn't know it was on the menu," James mumbled and then felt embarrassed for admitting he didn't know what items were on his own restaurant menu.

James excused himself from the table. That was the last straw. How dare they change the menu without consulting with him first. Maybe Dominidor talked to Hoku about it. It seemed she made independent decisions about the kitchen and dining room in her spare time. He stormed into the kitchen.

"Who changed the menu?" James ground his teeth and tried to keep from shouting. "Why aren't we serving chicken luau tonight? Where's Dominidor?"

Tatiana just stared at him, mouth agape.

"Where is the chef?" he repeated.

"In the hospital, sir, Mr. Westerman, sir."

"And were you left in charge?"

"I had help, sir. Everyone helped."

At that moment, Roselani walked up behind him, clasped his arm, and said firmly, "Let's walk, James."

She led him toward the service door and took him onto the walkway by the beach while she relayed the whole story about Dominidor's attack, his scheduled surgery and that several of the employees came in to help cover the duties.

James asked, "Why wasn't I consulted about all of those people working overtime?"

"You were not here, so the staff handled it. Tatiana, Hokulani, Keoni, and several others. You should be proud of them, James. They put together a wonderful menu with very little notice."

"And the cost? How much overtime will I have to pay?"

"No overtime. No extra costs. No one expects pay when we have an emergency in our Breezeway *'ohana*. It is what you do for family."

James tried to listen to her words. The cool breeze off the ocean helped him to relax a little. "I can't believe anyone works for free."

"Many of us have worked together for a number of years. We know each other's moods and disappointments. We support one another at the Breezeway. Wouldn't you want your family to help you out in an emergency?"

"Sure," he mumbled, "David would. I wouldn't hold my breath waiting for my father to show up."

"I'm sorry to hear that, James. But here, we are *'ohana*. And you are now part of our family, even when you are disappointed in us," Roselani said, and then changed the subject. "Don't you want to know how Dominidor is?"

James hung his head. "I'm sorry. I should've asked. How is he?"

"He will be fine, but he needs at least six weeks off work to recover."

"What will I do without him?"

Roselani answered, "You should march into the kitchen and apologize to Tatiana. And then, James, you should let her run the kitchen."

He nodded and headed back to the kitchen with Roselani.

"Tatiana," James called. "Roselani explained the situation to me and I'd like to ask you to step into Dominidor's position while he recovers. Are you willing?"

Roselani cleared her throat.

"And, I apologize for raising my voice with you."

"Apology accepted, Mr. Westerman, sir. I'll do whatever I can to make the kitchen run smoothly."

"Come to my office tomorrow so that we can make a plan for Dominidor's absence."

Roselani patted James's hand and walked him back to the table. "Thank you for lending us the boss, Mr. Caruso. We wanted his opinion on the barbecue sauce before we served his friend. Enjoy your dinner and the show."

James admired the way Roselani helped him save face in front of Stanley. If only her daughter were so considerate. Hoku hadn't even contacted him about the staffing problem in the kitchen, let alone include him in the solution. When he decided to choose her as the co-manager, he hadn't bargained for her obstinacy.

"Oh, baby," James heard Stanley utter.

James realized Hoku was on stage. "Beg your pardon?" James asked.

"The hula girl. Available?"

"Mine," James shot back.

Chapter Eight

James arrived at the office the next morning at just after seven, and found Hoku already at her desk on her cell phone. He tried not to stare when she closed her eyes and held the phone away from her ear. "Kawika, aren't you going to ask how your daughter is?"

James tried to busy himself, but couldn't help but hear Kawika's angry voice reverberate through the receiver.

Hoku persisted. "Regardless, she's still sick. I'm taking her to the doctor today and you'll need to write her a note for her absences from school."

James didn't like to see those furrowed brows so early in the day. It could only mean trouble.

"I'll talk to you after we get home from the doctor," Hoku said. She looked at James. "Aloha."

James thought about what Roselani said to him the night before. "Aloha, Hoku. How is Dominidor this morning?"

"He's scheduled for surgery around ten. Mom will go to the hospital to keep Maricar company." She paused. "*Mahalo* for asking."

"Your mom gave me a crash course in Sensitivity 101."

"I wondered."

We do need to talk about what happened yesterday in the kitchen."

Hoku squared her shoulders.

"The staff did a great job of covering for Dominidor and his family. Roselani explained that everyone pitched in as volunteers. I'm not sure that would happen at any other property we manage."

James watched as her shoulders relaxed.

"Tatiana took charge and organized all of us." Hoku said.

"Yes, I spoke with her about taking over Dominidor's duties in his absence. She'll be in today to discuss the staffing and menu options with me—I mean us."

Hoku nodded.

"One more thing, Hoku. I know you handled the situation, but I have to say that you should've at least notified me. I took my cell phone and checked messages after my workout."

"It didn't occur to me—"

"But it should occur to you. I thought we were trying to live up to our management agreement and make big decisions together?"

She looked down at the floor. "I don't have your cell number. I deleted it from my phone."

"I see."

"I was angry."

"And, of course, everyone here has your number in case of emergency. I'll have to give my number to the supervisors and the front desk. I neglected to do that. I thought…well, anyway, you need to have my number as a business partner."

"Of course. Let me program it in right now and then we should go over our schedule for the day. I have to take Lei to a doctor's appointment this morning, but that should only take an hour or so."

"Is she sick?"

"Yes. It's probably just the flu, but I want to get her checked out. She seems tired all the time and one of the girls at school has mono, so we want to rule that out. Or, to be exact, I want to rule that out. Kawika …well, let's just say, Kawika is not able to take care of her right now."

"So you are filling in the parental duties."

"I have since Janice died."

"Lei's lucky to have you." *Lucky to have someone who fills in as the mother,* he thought.

He hadn't thought about his mother in a long time. He couldn't remember what she looked like, but he remembered when he sat on her lap, she smelled of lilacs and he felt safe in her arms. James couldn't recall ever sitting on his father's lap or receiving a hug from him. It was always "buck up and be a man" even when he was three years old.

"James? Are you okay?" Hoku asked.

"Yeah. Probably just need another cup of coffee."

****

Two hours later, Hoku cradled her niece on the couch at home. She picked up her phone and called James. "I won't be back until show time. Something's come up."

"Is everything okay? Are you okay? You sound upset."

"It's a family thing. I won't be able to meet with Tatiana. You go ahead and meet with her yourself." Hoku hung up and ran her hands up and down Lei's back.

Lei hugged her knees to her chest and buried her face in the crook of her arms. Hoku tried to sooth her. "Hush now. I'll go with you to tell your dad."

"I didn't mean to!" Lei cried. "He said he loved me, and I believed him."

"Maybe he believed he did love you." *Like I believed I might love James*, she thought.

Hoku arranged to meet with Kawika later at his house. Nothing she said could convince Lei to go with her, so she went alone. Maybe it was best. Hoku didn't expect Kawika would maintain his composure when he first heard the news. At least she had a solution to propose to him.

She knocked, let herself in, and found Kawika at his dining room table with a drink in his hand. Hoku hugged him.

"If you want to talk about Lei coming back home, the answer is no. I really don't want to see her," he said without looking up. He looked just like he did the day Janice died.

"Honestly, Kawika. Why are you so upset with her?"

"Did you know about the boyfriend?"

"I found out a couple of days ago."

"Did you know that they were having sex, in my house, while I was at the office?"

Hoku laid her hand on his arm. "I had no idea, Kawika. I thought she was staying home because she was sick."

"That's what she told me, too. I trusted her to tell me the truth. And then, yesterday, I came home at lunchtime to get some papers for a meeting, and I saw this strange car in our drive. I didn't recognize the car, so I ran into the house to make sure my baby was safe, and there they were..." He grimaced and pointed to the couch.

"Oh, Kawika." Hoku wiped tears from the corners of her eyes. "I'm so sorry."

"I yelled for him to get the hell out of my house. I threatened to kill him if he ever came around again." Kawika's voice cracked. "He laughed at me, Hoku. He just laughed as he gathered up his clothes and walked right past me to go out the door."

"How awful."

"I kicked her out, Hoku. I don't think I can stand to look at her after what she did."

"She'll stay with me," Hoku said.

The silence in the room gathered around Hoku while she tried to figure out how to tell her brother the reason she'd come. "Look, Kawika, there's something else you need to know."

"How can there be more?"

"She's three months pregnant."

Kawika slammed his fist into the table. "That son-of-a-bitch. I'll kill him."

Hoku laid her hand on his. "I have a solution."

Kawika pushed her hand away. "You can't undo what's been done. If I ever see that bastard again, I swear—"

"Kawika, listen to me. Lei is not the first teenager to get pregnant, but we are her family and we'll do what we need to do to support her. This isn't easy for her, either."

He poured another full tumbler of whiskey and drank it down.

Hoku kept talking, "I want to raise the baby. Lei will still go to college, as we planned."

"You can't raise her baby."

"Why not? I want a family and this way Lei can be free to grow up without the responsibility a baby would place on her."

"She ought to be held accountable. She ought to pay for her own mistakes."

"Don't you want what's best for her? She's your daughter, Kawika."

"Not anymore." He bolted from the room.

Hoku's hands shook, and she forced herself to take deep breaths. She prayed for Kawika to find it in his heart to forgive Lei. She got in her car and drove to the Breezeway. Right now, she needed to hear what her mom would advise. Hoku was out of ideas.

She knocked on her mom's door and called out as she entered, "Aloha, Mom. It's Hokulani."

"*Hele mai*. What a nice surprise."

"I need to talk with you."

"Is this about the employee evaluations? I am hearing grumbling about that and wondered if you talked to James about how it affects our *'ohana*."

"It's something we have to work through, Mom, but that's not why I stopped by."

"Why then? Is everything okay?"

"It will be."

Hoku took her mom's hand. "Mom, Lei is *hapai*. She doesn't want to be, but she knows that carrying the child to term is the right thing to do."

"*Hapai*? I did not know she had a boyfriend."

"I don't think he's in the picture at this point. Kawika ran him off when he found him at the house with Lei."

"How is she?"

"Experiencing a lot of morning sickness and fatigue, but the doctor told her it was normal."

"So, she has seen a doctor?"

"Yes. I took her in for blood work and the doctor took a urine sample."

"And Kawika?"

"Upset. Angry. Mad at the world. He kicked Lei out yesterday, so she's staying with me. And, Mom…I proposed to Lei that she allow me to raise the child."

"And you feel ready to do this?"

"Yes, I am. Lei's not ready to raise a baby and Kawika is not prepared to raise another child. I always thought I would have a child by now, so this is a blessing for me."

Roselani hugged her daughter. "You are doing the right thing, Hokulani. You know I will help."

"I know you will."

"Where is Lei now? I would like to see her."

"She's resting at my house. She didn't want to tell you herself. She's so afraid of disappointing you."

"Then I will just have to make sure she knows I love her no matter what. I will get some things together and keep her company while you do your show tonight."

"*Mahalo,* Mom."

Hoku made one more stop before she drove back up the hill to check on Lei. The zesty aroma that wafted from the kitchen had to be Tatiana's special barbecue sauce.

"Mmm, smells *ono*," Hoku said as she entered through the service the door.

"The barbecue chicken seems to be selling. Mr. Westerman told me in our meeting today that I had the freedom to try a few new recipes."

Hoku said, "About that. Sorry I missed the meeting. I took Lei to the doctor."

"And?"

"Turns out she's *hapai.*"

"You don't seem upset."

"I think she'll let me *hanai* the child as long as her boyfriend doesn't want to marry her."

"Oh, Hoku." She wiped her hands on her apron and hugged her friend. "A baby."

"I want this more than anything, but first we have to make sure the father will give up his rights."

"Keep me posted. I hope it all works out for you."

****

James looked at the time again. Nine. Hoku didn't do any work yesterday and she wasn't in the office again this morning. After three days of intermittent work, James decided he couldn't very well wait for a woman who had a family crisis almost daily.

He picked up the phone and called Westerman Designs. "Marta?"

He talked to his friend and occasional lover about his latest acquisition and asked if she could come right away. "The lobby and dining room have this sort of hieroglyphics theme going on in brown and black."

He listened to her familiar laugh and remembered how easy it was to be around her. In all the years they worked together, she'd never once been late for a meeting.

Hoku came through the door and mumbled an apology. She rustled through some papers on her desk and announced that she had some family business to attend to and she would be back later.

"Hoku, we have work to do. What about the bids for the roofing job? Will you be able to get those out today?"

"I don't know, James. I told you I have a family situation to deal with."

"It was your family that insisted on co-management. Short of someone dying, I need to have you here to help make decisions. Is someone dying?"

"Go to hell." She grabbed her bag and left.

James watched her and the day's work go out the door. He really couldn't operate like this. Ever since she found out he was the investor, she'd been unpredictable. One minute she was charming and the next a viper.

How different she was from easygoing Marta who understood the importance of business and conversation without all the drama. Add to that Marta's willingness to sleep with him with no strings attached, and he wondered what he ever saw in Hoku. If Hoku couldn't take time to help manage the Breezeway, then he would just have to manage solo. That suited him just fine.

By noon, James scheduled computer training for the staff, released the notice for bids for the roofing job, and scheduled a meeting with Keoni to tighten up the expectations of the pool and landscaping staff. He thought Keoni sounded surprised by the request for a meeting, but too bad. It was time to get this place shaped up if he hoped to beat David in the family competition. He needed to refocus on business and stop thinking about Hoku.

James decided to take some of his own data on the pool attendants and landscaping crew. He took his iPad out to the pool area and timed how long it took to trim the hedges, and how often the staff stopped to talk to people.

From the pool area, James caught sight of Hoku as she rushed up the walkway toward the kitchen door. James followed her to find out, once and for all, what was so important that she couldn't perform her duties. He stopped short at the service entrance to the kitchen. He could hear Hoku talking to Tatiana. "Mom and I just got out of a meeting with Kawika."

"About the baby's father?"

She's pregnant. James's heart sank. *That's the family situation.*

"Lei agreed to let me adopt the baby on condition that the father doesn't change his mind and decide to marry her. Kawika decided to force this guy's hand and serve papers to see where he stands."

James almost revealed himself with his audible sigh of relief. *Hoku's not pregnant, Lei is.*

"Do you know how to find him?"

"Lei gave us his full name and Kawika already confirmed where he works. It was all Mom and I could do to convince Kawika to stay away from him. I really think my brother could hurt this guy."

"Can't blame him for that."

"I'm trying not to get my hopes up too high, but I pray he'll sign the papers to give up any claim to the child."

"And you're sure you want to raise a baby alone?"

"What choice do I have? I'm ready to start a family, and I don't have a man in my life."

"Sweetie, don't give up on men just because of what happened with Martin. What about James? I thought maybe you'd work things out with him."

"It turns out he's just like Martin. He's not nearly as interested in building a relationship as he is in winning a business competition with his brother. Both men wanted one thing from me."

"Maybe this competition is not such a bad thing."

"It's a silly rich boys' game. Daddy rewards whoever improves the profit margin the most on the property he manages."

"I hate to say it, Hoku, but won't an improvement on the profit margin of the Breezeway be a good thing? I mean, your family was at risk of losing the business before James invested."

"Yeah, it's a good thing to improve our business, it's just that—"

"It's just that you thought you had a chance with James, right?"

"Past tense, Tatiana. Kawika was right. I should not have involved myself with a business partner, and especially one from the mainland. Not that we were involved. I mean, there were definitely feelings I haven't had since Martin."

Feelings? James beamed. *So she does have feelings for me.*

"Then why is it a bad thing?" James cheered at Tatiana's persistence. "If you have feelings for him, don't keep pushing him away."

"Everything's changed. Right now, I need to concentrate on Lei and the baby. There isn't really time for a man."

James hurried around the building before Hoku left the kitchen. He knew he shouldn't listen to her private conversations. He should've walked away, and yet, after only three minutes, he understood Hoku better than ever before.

She admitted she felt something for him. He just needed to figure out a way to help Hoku renew those feelings.

Chapter Nine

James felt rather smug as he settled himself behind his desk. Sure, he needed to figure out *how* to win Hoku back, but he had a chance. He regretted what he said to her just before she walked out.

Hoku entered the office, said she was ready to work on the bids and asked if he'd print out a template for her.

James didn't quite know what to do. He'd taken care of that bit of business while she was out of the office all morning. He remembered what he'd overheard about him and relationships. "Is everything okay?"

She looked at him and nodded, "All taken care of."

"Good. That's good."

"So, do you have time to go over the templates with me?"

"Hoku, here's the thing. I took care of the request for bids this morning."

"I see. What else did you do while I was out of the office?"

"I took some data on Keoni's crew."

"Why did you do that? I thought we were going to let Keoni fill in his evaluation sheets for his crew."

"What if I told you it's mostly good news?"

"All right. I suppose we should look at the data since you gathered it."

James pulled up a chair to sit beside her. "Hoku, are you sure you're okay?"

"It's nothing I can't handle." She reached for the data sheet.

When they completed the data analysis, James announced he'd arranged for one of the Westerman Design team members to fly in to meet with them and get some ideas for the lobby renovations. He didn't reveal the person was Marta. He would cross that bridge later.

"Fine. Shall we talk about our vision before we meet with them?"

"Her. Just the lead is coming."

"How soon will she be here?"

"Two days. We should plan to meet with her that day."

"And will we have a chance to discuss our vision together before she arrives?"

"I thought maybe tonight, after your show, we could sit in the lobby and talk about it."

"That sounds like a good idea. I'll see you after the show."

That's more like it, thought James.

Later that evening, Roselani seated James at his favorite table near the stage. When she delivered his mai tai in a clear iced tea glass without the paper umbrella or fruit kabob, James looked at her and winced. "It's just not the same is it?"

"No, it is not, James. I wanted you to see how ordinary this drink is when served in a plain glass. This is a drink for someone who just wants to drink, not someone on vacation trying to enjoy themselves."

"I'm sorry about the other night when I was with Stanley. I've run businesses all over the country, and I've never had to learn so much about local nuance before."

"I am glad you see that, James. But, all in all, you are doing fine."

"Not where your daughter is concerned. I can't seem to get through one day without a disagreement with her."

"Her mind is preoccupied with Lei and the baby."

James acted surprised. "Baby?"

"I am surprised Hokulani did not tell you. Lei is *hapai* and Hokulani offered to *hanai* the child."

"What is *hanai*?"

"To adopt."

"Who will help her raise the child?"

"Oh, we will all help, but Hoku will be the recognized mother."

"I see."

"You may be new to the Breezeway family, James, but you are still part of our *'ohana*. You should know what is affecting people's moods."

She fluttered away to seat more guests. James sipped on his drink and thought about Roselani's acceptance of him, despite his mainland business ways. He decided right then he would listen to what Hoku had to say about the Breezeway renovations. For the first time in his life, he had the chance to be part of a family that behaved like a family. His father and brother always treated him like one of the guys, just another buddy, and he rather liked the idea that Roselani considered him part of the Breezeway family.

When Hoku started her solo hula, he hungered for the feel of her lips on his. He was sure, once again, that he could win her over, but not the way he originally thought. His normal charm hadn't worked on her. He was determined to do almost anything to make her see that he wanted her because he couldn't imagine life without her.

It was time for the audience participation set. The announcer's voice quieted the crowd. "Tonight we have a special surprise for you. Please put your hands together for Roselani Kawelu, the Kona Breezeway Inn's First Lady."

Roselani took the microphone. "The Kona Breezeway Inn is pleased to introduce, all the way from Boston, our new co-manager, Mr. James Westerman. James, will you join the dancers on the stage?"

James walked up the stairs and within an instant, six hula dancers surrounded him. Hoku brushed by his ear and said, "Mom's idea."

A raucous drumbeat started and the dancers swept around him and encouraged him to dance. They turned to the audience and pouted. "Who can show him how it's done?" the announcer called out.

Five male dancers hopped onto the stage with them and partnered up with all of the females except Hoku. She looked at the audience, shrugged her shoulders, took James by the hand and placed him in front of her. Hoku positioned her hands on the crests of his hips and he grasped hers.

James followed the slow, deliberate beat of the drum and pushed his hips one way, and then the other, in time with Hoku. He'd give anything to have her alone right now. When the tempo picked up, Hoku's hips shimmied so rapidly, he couldn't keep up with her gyrations or his own increased need to be with her. Before he knew it, Hoku reached for his hand and helped him take a bow. The audience went wild as James took his seat. He sat through the rest of the show with renewed hope that Hoku would give him a second chance.

After the show, Hoku joined him in the lobby. "I hope we didn't embarrass you too much."

"Quite the contrary. I love to dance with you." James held back his inclination to take her in his arms and hold her. Instead, he turned the conversation to the renovations.

"I've thought a lot about the lobby, Hoku, and I wonder what attracts you to the brown tones."

"Brown was a preferred color in old Hawai'i. I feel the lobby should be inviting without distracting from the natural beauty that surrounds us."

She took James's arm and turned him to face the lawn. "Remember when we talked about what you see when you enter the lobby? The registration desk is to the side, but mostly you see right out to the grounds and the ocean."

He liked that she stood close to him. He'd try to keep from arguing with her. "I see your point. I'm not sure I can imagine what would change if we stay with the brown tones."

"I don't know why it has to change. Fresh paint, yes, and replacing the furniture makes sense, but I would hate to see anything in the lobby distract from the view."

"Okay, so your vision is to keep with the old Hawai'i theme."

"Are you able to support that idea?"

"Would you be willing to have the designer show us an array of old to modern looks before we decide?" James asked.

"As long as she includes some old Hawai'i, I'm okay with that," Hoku said. "I should go." She headed toward the dressing room.

"Hoku, wait," James called as he jogged to catch up. "Will you take a walk with me? We need to talk."

****

At that moment, Hoku wished they weren't partners. Maybe things would be different then. A walk wouldn't hurt anything. She removed her shoes and headed for the beach. She could feel James behind her.

"I've been wrong," he said.

"About what?"

"I've been such a jerk about your family situation. Roselani told me about the baby."

"Hmm."

"She also told me about your offer to raise the child."

"It's not unusual in Hawai'i for a relative to take on the responsibility of a baby. Lei wants to go to college, and I want her to be able to finish being a child before she raises a child."

"And do you want a baby?" he asked.

"Very much. I thought I'd have a baby myself before now, but that didn't work out."

"I'm sorry, Hoku. The guy who hurt you must be one ignorant bastard."

"At least that bad."

"You know, I never thought much about having a family until I met you."

James reached for her hand, brought it to his mouth, and kissed it lightly. "Hoku, you have changed me into a man who wants to be married and have babies, and live in a house where I come home from work and trip on toys."

Hoku squeezed her eyes shut and whispered, "I want that, too."

James lifted her chin and brushed his lips against hers. The dormant fire within her erupted as she pressed her body against his. She clamored for his hungry mouth and fumbled for his groin. Hoku wrapped her arms around his neck and led him to a coconut grove where she leaned against the trunk of a coconut palm, unzipped his trousers, and shimmied out of her panties. His erratic breathing matched her own as she guided him into her. James mirrored the frantic thrusting of her pelvis.

Hoku pressed on James's rear until he slipped from her and his mouth possessed hers once again.

James touched her cheek with the back of his hand. "You're amazing, Hoku. When can I see you again?"

"Tomorrow night? I'll have Lei stay at Mom's."

"Will you astonish me with more of your agility?"

She kissed him deeply, hungrily, and then whispered in his ear, "Only if you say please."

When Hoku got home, she saw a familiar music box on the coffee table, and Lei asleep on the couch. *Mom must have brought the music box for the baby*, she thought.

The baby! What was I thinking? Hoku covered Lei with a blanket and tiptoed into her bathroom where she stripped down and stepped into the shower. She stood under the stream of hot water for a long time to let it rinse away any remnants of James.

Hoku felt ashamed that she had unprotected sex after what Lei was going through. She'd never been so impulsive in her life. She glared at her reflection in the mirror and vowed she was finished with James once and for all.

Relief washed over Hoku when she let herself into the office the next morning and realized James wasn't there. She sat at her desk and followed her handwritten directions to access the business email account James insisted she have set up. There was a message from James. *Probably just checking to make sure I know how to do this*, she thought.

"Change of plans—the designer arrives mid-morning today instead of tomorrow. I want to drive her around to help her get a feel for the island. If you need anything, call. I look forward to seeing you tonight for the agility workout."

In a frenzy, Hoku stabbed at the delete key. Nothing happened. She had no idea who might have access to this message. How could James have written such an incriminating email? She couldn't remember how to delete messages, and she wanted this one completely negated. She pulled out the manual and pushed buttons until she finally figured out how to put the message in the trash. With that done, she shut off the computer and cursed James under her breath.

Hoku walked to the lobby and checked at the desk to see if anyone signed up for her class on weaving *lauhala* leaf baskets. There were three on the list, so she went outside with her clippers and trimmed enough of the long slender leaves to make small baskets. As she handled the natural fibers, she started to relax. By the time class ended, she could think straight again.

It occurred to her that she still needed to ask her mom to invite Lei to dinner so that she could speak privately with James when he showed up that evening. She practiced a speech to let James know they'd made a mistake, an error in judgment. She felt so foolish. She should never have allowed herself to be lured into sex. *Unprotected sex, for crying out loud. What would Lei think if her auntie got pregnant because she didn't have enough sense to use protection?*

****

James showered and shaved. He couldn't help but imagine how Hoku's breasts would feel against his chest.

He shivered in anticipation of exploring new areas of her body. James forced himself to calm down so that he could dress in the khaki shorts, aloha print shirt, and sandals he bought especially to show Hoku that he could dress like a local guy.

He grabbed the chilled bottle of wine and the tropical floral bouquet and jumped in his rental car to head inland.

At the last minute, James stopped at a drugstore to purchase condoms. He preferred not to wear them, but he would if Hoku wanted him to. *Yesterday*, he thought, *she didn't seem concerned.*

James followed the handwritten directions Hoku had given him last night. He took a deep breath and knocked on the door. When Hoku finally answered the door, she was dressed in loose slacks and a button-down shirt. He noticed she'd buttoned the shirt higher than normal and she wore her hair in a tight bun.

He stood at the threshold, holding the wine and flowers. He leaned to kiss her, but she turned her head so that the kiss landed on her cheek.

"Come in, James," she said.

"These are for you." He handed her the flowers. "If you get me a corkscrew, I'll open the wine, unless you have something else planned."

"I made iced tea. Excuse me while I get a vase for the flowers."

James followed her into the kitchen and wrapped his arms around her from behind and nibbled at her ear. "I missed you today," he said.

"We need to talk." Hoku replied.

"Have I done something wrong?"

"No, not exactly."

Examining her gorgeous face, the face of someone whom he thought he could trust, he furrowed his brow. "I don't understand. I thought last night was special."

"Last night shouldn't have happened, James. We were as impulsive and irresponsible as a couple of teenagers."

Why would she initiate sex one day and spurn him the next?

He glared at her. "Last night, you took me to a coconut grove and seduced me, and tonight you won't look me in the eye?"

"I seduced you?"

"Who unzipped my pants, Hoku? Who led me to the coconut grove?"

"I was doing you a favor. You were so hard, I thought you'd explode."

"Don't do me any more favors." James stormed through the house, and let himself out with a new resolve to be done with her.

****

At five the next morning, Hoku looked at herself in the mirror, got an ice pack and went back to bed. She hoped the ice would help take the puffiness from her eyes. She had to pull herself together before it was time to go to the office.

Yesterday, she convinced herself James was to blame for everything that happened on the beach. But last night, when James wrapped his arms around her, the tug she felt between her legs was undeniable. She knew now what happened on the beach was mutual. She wanted him that night. She still did.

Hoku pressed the ice packs on her eyelids. James didn't need to know she'd been crying. She needed to do a good job for the family, get through the meetings with the Westerman designer, make plans for Lei and the baby, and figure out a way to help Kawika understand that he couldn't just shut out his daughter.

And most of all, she needed to make it through one day at a time in the office. *Just one day, and then the next*, she told herself. But even ice couldn't soothe the sting from her fresh tears.

Chapter Ten

When Hoku entered the office, James did not even acknowledge her presence. She wasn't sure what she expected from him, but she knew what she expected from herself. She needed to do the job her family trusted her to do.

"What time are we meeting with the designer?" she asked, in as businesslike a voice as she could muster.

James gleamed. "Marta arrives at ten."

"Marta? Like the Marta you sleep with?"

"Like the Marta who is the lead for the Westerman Design Team. She's very good at what she does."

"Hmm. Very good at what exactly? Isn't she the friend with benefits?"

"Do you really want to go down that road? After last night, I'm quite clear that you're not ready or willing to have a relationship with me, so I don't feel particularly inclined to have a conversation with you about my personal life."

"You are something else, James Westerman. You knew all along that it was Marta who was coming, and you chose not to tell me. I don't stand a chance of getting anything I want with the renovations now that your lover is in the picture. You chose a lousy way to get back at me."

"I promise to keep my hands to myself while she's here," he taunted.

"Do whatever you damn well please with your hands as long as you keep them off me!"

Hoku couldn't believe the nerve of James to bring in the one person she didn't want involved in their project. In Hoku's mind, the renovation project served as a sort of thermometer of how well she and James worked together. She'd hoped that the two of them could reach a compromise, and now this Marta woman would make recommendations based on her limited knowledge of Hawai′i.

And at night, well, who knew what Marta and James would find to do at night?

She was sorry that James selected her as the co-manager. She wasn't sure she could function. She knew that right now it was all she could do to breathe.

****

James sat in the office and pored over the sketches Marta presented to them. Hoku sat at her own desk and appeared disinterested. James tried again to engage her in the decision.

"What about this one?" James held up a sketch that displayed a large black lacquered table in the center of the lobby. Marta's sketch depicted a huge red vase, filled with four-foot tall flowers, posed on the table.

"First of all," Hoku spoke slowly, "when you originally showed me this design, I made it clear I didn't like it. It's a very sleek, modern look and not what the Breezeway should portray. The vase detracts from the ocean view, and I can't imagine what it would take to change the water and flowers."

"I think we should at least consider it," James said. "Marta called it contemporary."

"Honestly, James? Black lacquer? How on earth does slick, black lacquer have anything to do with the tropics?"

"Well, then? Which one do you like?" He set the offending sketch on his desk.

Hoku stood and walked to the front of James's desk. She flipped through the sketches for a few minutes, and then announced that she didn't care for any of them.

James wanted to scrap the whole project, but tried one more time to get Hoku's agreement on something. He held up the most tropical sketch he could find. "Could you live with any part of this one?"

"I suppose I wouldn't mind so much if it were brown. I like the look of sepia, like old photographs."

"But, how is brown different from what we have now? Marta says the brown is dull. Don't you think it's time to move the Breezeway into the twenty-first century?" He chuckled just a little as he looked at her.

"I don't give a damn what Marta thinks," she shot back. "I'm just telling you what I think and we agreed we would come to a mutual decision before we made any changes."

"Maybe we should ask someone else to choose between your favorite and my favorite."

"That's ridiculous. We should be able to reach an agreement."

"Yeah," James mumbled.

"I'd like to meet with Marta to show her some photos of old Hawai'i." So far, Hoku had only met briefly with her.

"She flies out in two days. Are you sure you're not going to scratch her eyes out? You don't seem to like her much."

"She's the designer, not my enemy."

"I'll arrange a meeting for the three of us."

"All right. Ask if she can come at eight in the morning."

"I'll call her to confirm and let you know." James stood. "I hope we can come to a decision tomorrow, Hoku. I'm anxious to get the ball rolling."

****

Hoku poured her fresh cup of coffee down the drain and reached for the antacids. She reminded herself that she lived through the last two days and she could muddle through this one.

Hoku arrived at the Breezeway just before eight. James and Marta already sat side by side in the lobby, laughing and drinking coffee. Sketches covered the surface of all the side tables. Hoku chewed a couple more antacids and sat down on the other side of James on the couch.

Marta extended her hand.

Hoku reached across James to shake Marta's hand and mumble, "Aloha." She couldn't deny the yearning she felt as she took in the scent of James and felt his body heat. She scolded herself. She needed to focus on business or this blonde hussy would talk James into converting the Breezeway into something it was not.

The sepia photographs she took from her tote bag depicted Hawaiian royalty, petroglyphs, Polynesian tattoo patterns, hula implements, and whaling ships. "These photographs of the past help immerse people in a time before Hawai'i was part of the United States. I believe the muted colors in the lobby invite the natural colors of the landscape to dominate."

Marta leaned forward to take the photographs from Hoku. "So the feel you want is taking guests back in time?"

Hoku tried to explain further. "Yes. If we immerse our guests in old Hawai'i, they go away from here thinking they have gone to a foreign land without all the bother of passports."

Marta flipped through the photos and smiled. "Let's see what we can come up with." She swept stray blonde hair behind one ear as she stretched to reach across James's body for a sketch.

Flirt, Hoku thought.

"Let's see if we can use what we have already and come up with a compromise," Marta said.

James laid his hand on Marta's knee. "We've always been able to do business before, so I don't see why we can't make this work."

Oh my God, Hoku thought, *he's coming on to her right in front of me.*

"Excuse me," Hoku interrupted. "Marta, would you mind if I borrow James for a private conversation?" She stood and pasted on her showgirl smile. James followed her to their office.

"Remind me why this is the person you chose as the designer?"

"I already told you. I trust her because she's done a lot of work with our family. Marta is highly regarded in Boston as a top-notch designer."

"And what is your relationship to her?"

James kept a straight face. "I already answered you. My family—"

"I don't mean your business relationship."

James paused. "It's really not your business, is it? You're the one who refuses to acknowledge what happened between us."

"Oh, I acknowledge it all right, James. At least I have the good sense to call it for what it was—acting like lustful teens instead of business partners."

"I don't think of you as just my business partner. That night on the beach wasn't just lust. I thought it was the beginning of our life together."

Hoku looked at her shoes. She wanted to believe him. She just couldn't allow herself to. "I've already told you it was a mistake."

"So why do you care about my relationship with Marta?"

She wished he would stop confusing her with these questions. In her logical mind, she shouldn't care about Marta. So why did she? She had to say something to make him stop. "I don't care except if she is your lover, you may not be thinking about business and what's best for the Breezeway."

"She's not my lover."

"You know what, James? You decide. You know my preferences and I'm tired of discussing this. Go out there and plan to your heart's content with Marta. I simply can't be around the two of you another minute." She left the office for the sanctuary of the cultural center.

****

James went back to the lobby to tell Marta that they wouldn't be making a decision anytime soon.

"Lover's spat?" Marta asked.

"She just wants her own way and won't settle for anything else."

"Then give her that."

"Why?"

"Because it's obvious that you love this woman and you need to show her that you value her opinion." Marta said.

"Is it so obvious?"

"It may not be obvious to everyone, James, but I've known you a long time. If you want this woman, you'll have to treat her as though her opinion is golden."

"Can you come up with additional sketches based on the old Hawai'i theme she wants?"

"Can you get me some family photographs to work with? I think I have an idea that may satisfy Hoku."

"Why are you trying so hard to make this work, Marta?"

"Because, I want you to be happy."

James walked back down the hall to the office. He was surprised to see Hoku at her desk, and vowed to take it slowly and think before he spoke. For now, that meant he better keep quiet and take his cues from her.

"Where's Marta?" Hoku snipped.

He kept his voice even. "Working on a new concept for the lobby."

"Do you have anything else planned for today?"

Is this a trick question? James wondered. "I'd like to discuss a bonus for Tatiana for filling in as head chef. And we should probably plan our next department lead meeting. What about you?"

"First, I better check the roster for today's lei-making class and pick flowers and ti leaves if anyone signed up. I'll go check on that and then we can talk about Tatiana's bonus and plan the meeting."

When Hoku went to the lobby to check the class roster, James noticed a full-page newspaper ad for nursery furniture—crib, changing table, and dresser—on her desk. He noted the style numbers and gave the store a call. On a whim, he charged the three pieces of furniture and arranged for a special delivery early the next morning.

Hoku popped her head in the door and said she had a family of five signed up and she needed to prepare the materials.

James followed her out the door. "Would you teach me how to cut the flowers and ti leaves?"

Chapter Eleven

Hoku collected a basket and her tools from the cultural center. She showed James how to pluck the fragile plumeria blossoms from the trees, and how to selectively cut ti leaves from the sides of the plant so that the center stalk continued to grow. He followed her around, said little, and stayed for the class.

After class, Hoku asked, "Shall we go back to the office and get some work done?"

James suggested they make a list of things that needed accomplished and Hoku agreed.

"Let's give Tatiana her bonus check at the employee meeting," James said. "How about five hundred?"

"I think she'll be pleased with that. I can't wait to see the look on her face when she sees the check."

James continued, "What do you think would make the employee meetings productive?"

She scrunched her nose. "We won't be productive until the group learns to trust you. That happens through casual conversation, so I'd like to continue serving breakfast. And I'd like to open the meetings with a chant to remind all of us that we are in this together."

Hoku was surprised when James agreed, with no argument, so she went a step farther. "Could we share all the data from the evaluation sheets with the leads, and ask them to brainstorm ways to improve efficiency?"

"We could try it," James said.

Hoku smiled as they continued to make plans for the Breezeway.

That evening after her performance, Hoku sat on her lanai and picked at the plate of food Lei made for her. She could see James tried to make the co-management work. *Like mom and dad*, she thought as she buried her face in her hands, *except we're only business partners.*

Hoku couldn't sleep, even though she felt exhausted. She couldn't eat, even though her mom baked her bread pudding with caramel sauce. And she couldn't stop thinking about James, even though she was the one who said they couldn't have a personal relationship.

After another fitful night, Hoku wiped the sleep from her eyes and pattered into the kitchen to make coffee and get breakfast ready for Lei. The loud knock on her front door startled her. She peeked through the window and saw two guys on her stoop and a delivery van in her drive.

She shook her head. *Must be at the wrong place.*

"Delivery for a Hokulani Kawelu," said the guy with the clipboard when she opened the door.

"There must be a mistake. I didn't order anything."

"The order says to deliver to a Hokulani Kawelu at 7:30 a.m."

She looked at the logo on the delivery van. "May I see what it is?"

When the van door opened, Hoku burst into tears. "The nursery furniture."

"Should we bring it inside?"

"Yes. Of course. I'm sorry I cried."

"No worries. Pregnant women cry a lot."

"But, I'm not...Who paid for this?"

"Don't know. We're just the delivery guys."

She gave them a generous tip and ran her hands over the top of the dresser, then the changing table, and finally the crib. She wiped away her tears and called her mom. "I just had the most wonderful surprise, and I suspect you're behind it."

"What are you talking about, Hokulani?"

"The nursery furniture was delivered just now. It's exactly the style I showed you yesterday."

"All three pieces?"

"Yes, Mom. All three pieces. They're perfect."

"I wonder who paid for that?"

"Didn't you?"

"No, sweetie. As much as I would like to take credit, it wasn't me."

"I wonder who, then?"

Hoku got ready to go to the Breezeway. As soon as she walked into the office and saw the furniture ad on her desk, she knew. She picked up the newspaper and looked at James. The slight grin on his face grew to a full-fledged smile. Tears pooled in her eyes and her mouth fell open, but no words spilled out.

"Do you like it?" James tipped his chair backward.

"Oh, James, it's perfect. But how can I accept such an expensive gift?"

"Because it's for the baby. Please just accept it."

She walked around his desk and gave him a hug. "*Mahalo nui loa.*"

Hoku forced herself to step away from him.

****

James stopped by the kitchen mid-morning. "Smells delicious."

Three pineapple upside-down cakes, fresh from the oven, sat on the counter. "It always does. It doesn't seem to matter how many of these I bake, I always love the smell when I take them from the oven. Would you like a slice, Mr. Westerman?" Tatiana asked.

"I would. Thanks. And please call me James."

Tatiana reached for the hot pads and turned the cake pan upside down and tapped. A perfect cake sat on the serving platter. Tatiana sliced a generous piece and put it on a dessert plate for James.

"Would you join me in the dining room?" he asked.

She followed James to the empty room and sat across from him at a booth. "Tastes as good as it smells." He took a few more bites before he said anything else.

"I wanted to talk to you about a couple of things," he began. "First of all, thank you so much for keeping the kitchen together in Dominidor's absence. You've done an excellent job at stepping up to the main chef position."

"I'm glad I could help. I've always had such high regard for Uncle Dom, but after filling in for him, I appreciate him even more."

"I also want to ask you a few questions about Hoku."

Tatiana folded her hands. "Hoku?"

"Yes. I know you are close friends so I hoped you could give me some help."

"I'm not sure I should talk about Hoku without her knowledge," she answered.

"I think you misunderstand. I just want to know some of her favorite things so I can get her a birthday gift."

"Oh, well, according to Hoku, you just gave her a very generous gift. She is so grateful for the furniture. She thought she could only buy the crib."

"That gift was for the baby. I want this gift to be just for her."

"Let me think…Her favorite colors are green, brown, and blue. She likes Hawaiian music, of course, and flowers. Anything that depicts old Hawai'i, or hula. Does that help?"

"It does. Thank you and keep up the good work."

James left the kitchen and stumbled upon Hoku's afternoon *keiki* hula class. He didn't know how old the children were, but they seemed to follow Hoku's lead very well. He sat down on a bench and watched as Hoku instructed a move and the children tried it out. After an attack of the giggles, the small dancers tried to jiggle their knees and bend at the same time. Hoku was patient, but persistent. At the end of fifteen minutes, every child could perform the move. *She's a natural mother*, James thought.

****

It surprised Hoku to see James walk into the cultural center with a new ukulele.

"Keoni helped me pick it out," he said. He sat cross-legged on a *lauhala* mat and tried to strum it.

Hoku laid three more ukuleles on the mat, and sat down next to James to show him how to play the basic chords. His strumming was erratic, but he picked up the finger positions easily. Hoku loved that James started to attend the cultural classes. Watching him learn new things was her favorite. When he concentrated his hardest, his face scrunched up and his adorable dimple dominated his features.

James's face was in that position when the family of three came in for class. He just looked up and called out "aloha" while Hoku settled the students on the mats. The dad sat next to James and by the end of class they were able to play a three-chord duet of "*Ahi Wela*/Twinkle, Twinkle, Little Star".

Hoku felt as though she and James's routine benefited the Breezeway. Her only regret was that even though the business relationship stabilized, she'd destroyed any hope of a personal relationship.

Still, she had Lei to take care of and a baby to prepare for. Ever since Kawika confirmed that Roland wanted nothing to do with paying child support, and that he willingly signed away his paternal rights, she'd researched how to care for an infant. Hoku never envisioned her life with a baby and no husband, but she wanted so much to be a mother, she convinced herself it would be okay.

On Tuesday morning, James helped Hoku set the table for the department lead's meeting. Hoku just smiled when James greeted each of the four employees with an "aloha" and asked about their families.

Tatiana sat in for Uncle Dom. She brought James a piece of warm pineapple upside-down cake and got a hug in return.

After breakfast, Hoku stood to begin the meeting with a chant, and then led an activity where people gave the person next to them a compliment. James volunteered to go first and told Tatiana that he appreciated the way she organized the kitchen the day Dom went to the hospital. Tatiana told Keoni that she appreciated his sunny disposition and that his smile helped her get through some of her gloomiest days.

The compliments went all the way around the table until it was Hoku's turn to compliment James. She turned to him. Suddenly, tears welled up as she tried to speak. She sniffled, took a breath and said, "I appreciate the way you have embraced our culture."

James looked at her and smiled broadly. "*Mahalo*," he said.

James turned back to Tatiana and asked her to stand. "Hoku and I wanted to recognize Tatiana today by giving her a bonus check for stepping into the head chef position." He handed her an envelope.

Hoku regained her composure and urged, "Open it."

Tatiana just stared at the check and then gave James and Hoku each a hug. "This is enough to replace the plumbing in my bathroom. *Mahalo nui loa*."

Hoku loved being instrumental in spreading aloha. "And now, some good news for all of you. James and I want to try a new process to see how it goes. We'll try this monthly and if it works, we'll modify the evaluation forms so that we just collect the most valuable data in order to improve the Breezeway."

A thunderous clap shook the bandstand.

James presented the data packets to each of them, and as a group, they looked for trends. They listed one positive trend for each department and made suggestions for improvements in each department. The department lead chose one improvement from the list that they wanted to work on for the next month.

At the end of the meeting, James and Hoku walked back to the office together and settled into Hoku's ongoing computer training. She could use her email account and even download photos and attach them to messages. She still needed practice on how to use the spreadsheets, but she felt pleased she was better able to understand the financial end of the business.

Maricar stopped by the office to thank James for the extra two-week's pay he offered so she could stay home and take care of Dom. "*Mahalo* for helping us. I'm relieved to know that I can stay home and take care of Dom without worrying about money."

"You're welcome," James said. "I know trying to live off temporary disability must be tough. I figured what would help Dom the most was having his lovely wife at home with him."

Maricar chatted with Hoku for a few minutes about how Lei was doing and then left the office.

"Why didn't you tell me you were helping Uncle Dom and Maricar? That was a nice gesture, James."

"I'm trying," he said. "Aren't you the one who keeps telling me every decision can't be based on money?"

"That's me," Hoku answered. "Can we afford to spend that much extra money though?"

"We're doing okay."

She tried to word her next question without sounding sarcastic. "Good enough to win your father's competition?"

James asked, "Are you still angry about that?"

"Not angry. Curious. What would happen if you won?"

"I planned to start my own small investment firm. *Planned*," he emphasized. "Now I'm just trying to keep our heads above water so I can stay in Hawai'i."

"I'd like that," she admitted. *More than you know.*

Chapter Twelve

On the morning of her birthday, Roselani greeted Hoku in the lobby and gave her a triple orchid lei. "Happy Birthday, Hokulani. May this year bring you everything your heart desires."

"*Mahalo*. The lei is beautiful, Mom."

"Well." Roselani began to fidget. "I have many things to do before your party tonight. Oh, how I love a good party!" she exclaimed.

"I'll see you later." Hoku headed for the office.

James was at his desk writing something. He covered it up with his hands and grinned at her. "Aloha, Hoku." He rose to place a self-made ti leaf lei around her neck. "Happy Birthday." His hug was firm and the kisses on her cheeks were whispers of promises.

Hoku stretched her arms around his back. "*Mahalo*." She could have stayed in that position for the whole day, but instead, she patted his back and asked what was on today's agenda.

"Nothing pressing. I have one errand later today. I thought maybe we could take the day off."

She gave that some thought. "What a lovely idea, but what about your teleconference with Marta?"

"I did it early this morning."

"Have you two come to any decisions about the lobby?"

"As a matter of fact, we have."

She took a breath. "What did you decide?"

"You'll see. Not right now. Let's just take a drive after the *lauhala* weaving class. I'd like to take you to lunch at that little Thai place in Volcano. Unfortunately, we won't have time to visit Madam Pele."

"You're sure we can get away?"

"Your mother would prefer you were not here while she prepares for your party."

"Okay. It's a plan. Now, would you like to prepare the *lauhala* for our class?"

Hoku had two families in her class that day. James sat at the table next to a six-year-old and helped him lace the pliant leaves in and out. Hoku noted how patient he seemed with the little guy. She let her thoughts wander. *He'll make a good dad.*

****

James offered to drive, but Hoku insisted that he could take in the scenery better if she drove. *Like I'm looking at the scenery*, he thought. Just like the first time they made this drive, he had trouble viewing anything but Hoku's face.

He encouraged her to tell him stories of Pele and what it was like to grow up at the Breezeway. By the time they reached the Ka'u Desert, James had his hand over Hoku's on the gearshift. He didn't know how it could be possible for Hoku to be more beautiful than the first day he watched her float across the lobby, and yet she was.

During lunch, and all the way back to Kona, James tried to formulate the right words to let Hoku know how he felt. When she pulled into the parking lot of the Breezeway, he grabbed her hand before she could get out of the car.

"Hoku," he began, "I know it's your birthday, and I shouldn't bring up business, but I wonder how you think it's going?"

"I think we've figured out how to co-manage the Breezeway. I'm comfortable with you as my business partner. How about you?"

"Ditto." James lifted her hand to his lips and lightly kissed her fingertips, one at a time. "Do you think we have a chance to build a personal relationship?"

"I don't know, James. I'm still not sure we're right for each other. Anyway, I'm not sure I can concentrate on a relationship right now. Lei needs me and preparing for the baby takes time." She spoke faster now. "I don't know, James. I just don't know."

He held her hand tightly. "When are you going to put yourself first? When are you going to think about what you want?"

"I don't know," her voice cracked.

"Then let me help you decide. I don't know what else I can do to show you how much you mean to me. I want us to be married and raise Lei's child together. Kids should have two parents. I know, I grew up without a mother in the picture and I don't want that for this child. I'm telling you that I love you and I choose to invest in us."

"I don't know what to say. I need time. Please give me time." Hoku looked away.

"Okay. You're right. I don't want to spoil your birthday, but you have to know that I'm a changed man, and I have to know if you will choose us."

****

Kawika met Hoku in the lobby. "I want to give you my present before the party," Kawika said.

They sat down on the couch and Kawika pulled out a letter from the University of Washington. "This came for Lei. I don't know what it says, but it could be the acceptance or the denial letter. I felt so angry with her, Hoku. And now, this letter reminds me that she's young and just starting her life. I need to be the adult here and step up as her father. I'm going to invite her to move back home tonight. I miss her."

Hoku clung to her brother. "This is the best birthday present you could give me. *Mahalo,* Kawika."

"I'm not done. I also realize that I can sometimes be too protective of you. I'll never forgive Martin for the pain he put you through, but that doesn't mean I should impose rules on you about who you choose to date. If you're interested in James, don't let me stop you. You deserve to be happy. Will you forgive me for acting like a jerk?"

Hoku glowed when she and Kawika entered the dining room. Roselani greeted them and then put Kawika to work and sent Hoku to the kitchen to keep Tatiana company.

Lei came through the kitchen door. "Auntie, I'm so nervous. Is Dad here yet?"

"He is. Let me go get him so you two can talk before the party."

Hoku followed Kawika into the kitchen. He had a lei in one hand and a pair of scissors in the other. He cut the lei to acknowledge that this lei was for someone who was *hapai*.

Lei burst into tears. "Oh, Daddy, I'm so sorry."

He opened his arms to her, and she ran to him. Hoku brushed away tears as Kawika soothed Lei and invited her to come back home. Kawika handed Lei the envelope and she ripped it open. "I got accepted!" She jumped up and down. "I'm going to the University of Washington."

Hoku joined the guests in the dining room. Everyone she considered family was there—her mom, Kawika and Lei, her *hālau* dancers, and her Breezeway *'ohana*. She searched the room for the newest member of the *'ohana* and found James playing a video game with Tatiana's eight-year-old son. When she approached, Lucas told her that he beat Uncle Kimo three times.

"Uncle Kimo?"

"My mom told me to call him that," Lucas said.

"May I borrow Uncle Kimo?" Hoku asked.

She invited James to sit with her for the meal. "Is it a good thing to be called Kimo?" James asked.

"Yes. It means you've earned your Hawaiian name."

"Uncle Kimo. I like it," he said.

When the buffet line opened, James followed Hoku and asked her questions about what this dish was and what that was. By the time they sat to eat, he had a plate filled with local food.

"Eat up, Kimo," Hoku said.

At the end of the meal, Roselani stepped up to the microphone to announce that James had a special gift for Hokulani and invited her to sit on the stage. James approached the microphone with a flat bundle tied in aloha print fabric. He welcomed everyone and thanked them all for coming to help celebrate Hoku's birthday.

He laid the gift in Hoku's lap. She pulled the ribbon from the bundle and saw a sketch of a young woman leaning over a child on the beach with her gift of *mauli ola*, the breath of life.

Hoku stared at James.

"If you approve, these sketches will become a mural to decorate the lobby. No black lacquer tables or sleek designs. Just the mural and some couches where people can gather," he said.

Hoku held up each sketch, one by one, to share with her *'ohana*. The series of sketches told the history of the Kona Breezeway Inn: Hanalei and Roselani's wedding on the beach, the first building and luau grounds, Hanalei weaving ti leaf leis with his mother on the original lanai facing the Pacific, Roselani greeting guests in the lobby, Hoku dancing hula, and Kawika meeting Janice for the first time. They were all there—Uncle Dom preparing the luau pig, Maricar setting up the dining room, Keoni cutting open a coconut to share with guests, and Tatiana slicing a pineapple upside-down cake in the kitchen.

Hoku could barely see the last sketch as she wiped away tears. James handed her his handkerchief, and she dabbed at her eyes. The sketch was a family portrait. Roselani seated in a white wicker chair with Kawika and Lei behind her and to the left. Hoku was on the right cradling a baby wrapped in an aloha print blanket. There was an outline of a person beside her—someone taller. She looked up at James. He nodded.

Hoku set the sketches on the chair and wrapped her arms around James's neck. "I choose us," she whispered.

James held her while their Breezeway *'ohana* clapped and whistled. Then, Keoni handed James his ukulele, and Hoku sat back down. As James began to strum, Hoku suddenly knew what all of those meetings with her mom were about. He learned to play her favorite Hawaiian love song, "I'll Weave a Lei of Stars for You".

Hoku gazed into James's emerald green eyes as he serenaded her.

James handed the ukulele over to the bandleader while the band continued the song. He offered his hand to

Hoku, and she wrapped her arms around him and nuzzled her head into his chest.

After all the guests left the party, James took the old-fashioned metal key from his pocket and held it up. Hoku took it and led him to his room.

The first kiss was long and delicious. James nibbled at her ear and whispered how much he loved her, how good they would be together, and how he was ready to be a father to the baby.

He slowly unzipped her dress and eased it down over her hips. "What's this?" he asked her.

She could feel his fingertip trace the edges of her tattoo—a double-hulled sailing vessel.

"The *Hokulea*."

"Like the Hoku in your beautiful name?"

Hoku looked into his eyes. "Hoku means star. *Hokulea* means guiding star."

"Guide me," James whispered as he held her in his arms.

Made in the USA
San Bernardino, CA
29 July 2014

ABOUT THE AUTHOR
JACKIE MARILLA

Jackie Marilla writes contemporary romance with just a little spice. She published her first short story, ONLY ON VALENTINE'S DAY, with Books To Go Now in January of 2014.

Jackie lives on a farm in Hawai'i with her supportive husband, several feral cats, and a flock of hodgepodge chickens. When she's not at her desk writing, Jackie loves to visit her grown children and grandson in the Pacific Northwest, read, sew, and make lampwork glass beads. In a past life, she was an elementary school teacher.

Jackie is a member of the Romance Writers of America and the Greater Seattle Chapter.